PRAISE FOR **WILDFIRE**

"Those who think there are no women on the front lines fighting the devastating fires that annually scourge our forests should by all means take a look at Toni Draper's debut novel WILDFIRE. The nuts and bolts of fighting killer blazes and the camaraderie of those who battle them are both given Draper's knowledgeable attention, but WILDFIRE does not neglect the passionate hot spots in the human heart that are just as explosive but often more difficult to extinguish. Fire in the forests, bonfires in the heart: a fascinating read."

—ANN WADSWORTH, author of *Light, Coming Back*

"It is my pleasure to recommend this beautifully written book. I was completely hooked from the very first words and could not wait to read more. Having been a Wildland firefighter and Wildland Fire Operations Specialist for over 30 years, primarily in the Southwest, I commend Toni Draper on her efforts to tell this story so well. She does an amazing job of truly capturing the essence of Wildland Fire as if she had spent years on the Fireline herself. It's a story of courage and love that will warm the wildfire in your heart."

—BEQUI LIVINGSTON, Retired US Forest Service,
Southwestern Region, Fire Operations Health and
Safety Specialist, and creator of Fireline Fitness
and Women in Wildland Fire Boot Camp

TONI DRAPER

WILDFIRE

a novel

interlude ✦ **press** • new york

ISBN 13: 978-1-951954-07-9 (trade)
ISBN 13: 978-1-951954-08-6 (ebook)
Library of Congress Control Number: 2020946278
Published by Interlude Press
http://interludepress.com
BOOK AND COVER DESIGN BY CB Messer
BASE PHOTOGRAPHY FOR COVER ©Depositphotos.com/PiLens
10 9 8 7 6 5 4 3 2 1

interlude press • new york

For Cyndi,
without whose love and support
this *Wildfire* would never have ignited.

AUTHOR'S NOTE

I WROTE *WILDFIRE'S* FIRST DRAFT more than ten years ago. I always believed it had potential, but couldn't quite get it right, so I put it away where it collected dust and got on with life.

While I know many can and do teach and write simultaneously, when I was in the classroom, I never mastered that balancing act. Being an educator took all of my energy. I couldn't and didn't even think about writing again until I resigned my teaching position—coincidentally, right before the pandemic rocked our world with a seismic shift. Although I had secured a position in the regional office of another school district, the start date was pushed back, leaving me stuck at home with more time than I knew what to do with—*or did I?* The silver lining became evident.

I picked up my manuscript and finally saw what it was I didn't like about it. I re-wrote the ending along with a few other scenes and passages before sending my baby out into the publishing world where, thankfully, she was well-received and is now in your hands.

I hope you enjoy this, my debut novel, and welcome any words for me you might have. For feel-good phrases, I thank you from the bottom of my heart and in advance. With all the many choices out there in the book world readers have, I'm grateful to you for giving me and *Wildfire* a chance. Happy reading!

~ Toni

Some readers may find some of the scenes in this book difficult to read. We have compiled a list of content warnings which you can access at www.interludepress.com/content-warnings.

 PROLOGUE

BARELY VISIBLE AGAINST THE CAMOUFLAGING cones and decomposing needles of the fragrant forest floor, the small rodent sat back on its furry haunches and sniffed frantically at the thick unmoving air, its tiny whiskers twitching in the direction of the crackling of a nearby ponderosa pine—the burning sap, its agitation's source. A lightning strike had ignited a spark in the dehydrated branches of the towering evergreen, from which a growing flame now unfurled. Quietly and quickly the smoke spiraled upward from the top of the tree as the fire spread to the limbs of first one and then another, in a macabre and menacing dance, on its way to becoming nature's deadliest threat to the surrounding wilderness and its unsuspecting and unspoiled fauna and flora.

CHAPTER 1

JIMENA "MENA" MENDOZA, HER FACE blackened and streaked by soot and sweat, sat back on the heels of her Timberlands as she pulled up, ripped out and cut away small brush, plants, grass, and weeds. They had all turned brown and brittle due to a severe and early summer drought. One of a crew of fifteen, all men except for herself and another native Yuman, she had been called in to help clear a break up the ridge from the ravine, well in front of the fire. For the time being, beneath windless skies, it burned under control.

The raggedy red bandanna she used to cover and protect her mouth and nose from the choking smoke hung loosely around her neck, in contrast to a shiny, woven chain of gold. With a flick of her wrist, she yanked the cloth up and wiped away the perspiration that had beaded on her brow. Using the other hand, she swept aside onyx bangs that had been plastered flat against her forehead, from which sweat now trickled down. With a sigh and a groan, she stood to stretch her cramped legs and aching back.

No one knew a lot about Mendoza, other than the obvious to all. Although short in stature, what she lacked in height, she more than made up for in depth and strength of character and body. A quick thinker and quiet speaker, she preferred solitude to camaraderie and a book to a beer. Given the opportunity, she kept to herself, even amid a boisterous crowd. A very private person, she was a mystery to all. No one at the firehouse had ever seen her out and about with anyone else, so many let their imaginations spark and run wild, like the fires they fought to put out.

Rumor had it Mendoza didn't like men, and some said she didn't like people at all. She'd always gotten the impression the guys felt uneasy around her, like they didn't know how to be with her. She imagined she was different than many of the women they were used to, the one-night stands they often picked up in dive bars and honky-tonks. She'd heard the talk. Word had it that she related to the thrill and danger of nature's unpredictable, untamable dark side, perhaps because it reminded her of herself. *Let them wonder. A woman's gotta have a little mystery.* She smiled at the thought.

This season, which was just beginning, the crew hadn't seen much active fire, but that was all about to change now that they'd been called and moved north to the towering ponderosa pine forests. They were digging line, trying to stay ahead of the game. The *clink* of shovels as they were pushed into the forest's floor, striking small rocks along the way, took on the sound of a natural symphony of sorts. The men and women sunk, filled, and lifted their blades, scraping everything down to mineral soil in attempts to rid the earth of any and everything, including roots that could otherwise become fueling vegetation as the fire advanced. Their goal was to stop it in the three-foot wide dirt track they were creating.

Mena placed her palm on the characteristic rust-orange bark of the nearest stalwart pine. It stood so tall and straight. She then leaned forward and placed her nose along the protective outer surface of its mighty trunk and took a deep breath in. No one knew for sure why the tree gave off such a sweet aroma that many likened to vanilla, baking cookies, or even butterscotch. Backing her face away, she ran her hand over the bark that was split into big sections, much like the desert when it was deprived of water. She gave the evergreen one last pat and returned to the work at hand.

It took the rest of the morning for her crew to finish connecting their dirt track to an outcropping of large rocks that jutted out from the forest's floor and created a natural break in the landscape for a good thirty feet or so. On the other side of that divide, she resumed her work, along with the others. As they moved deeper into the thick of the stand, they mostly encountered needles, cones, and other fallen debris. They moved, scraped, and threw forward, always facing the way in which the fire would eventually come, just in case it surprised them and got there sooner than expected.

By sundown, they were all ready to call it a day.

Gonzalez, one of her fellow firefighters, said, "I don't know about you guys, but I am beat-down tired. All the bending and lifting and the stretching, first this way before twisting that... I guess I'm just getting too old for this type of work. I might have to call it quits after this season."

Mena commiserated with his pain.

After gathering their equipment, they headed back to the camp they'd earlier created and hurriedly grabbed a bite to eat so they could get some shut-eye. They were all too aware the sun would shine and call them forth again before they were physically well-rested enough to rise.

Mena had barely unrolled her bag and slid into place before her exhausted body demanded rest, urging her mind to follow. It was her stubborn heart that refused to give in, insisting in defiance that she be made aware of the date and its undying significance. She had always believed there was no such thing as coincidence, that everything that happened was, no matter how small, a part of her life's plan. She let the lull of her waking dream pull her like a slow-moving current into the past: from the day she'd stumbled upon Sydney's novel and the inexplicably burning impulsivity that had completely engulfed her to when she'd opened its cover to discover a link between the reader and writer that defied ignoring. No, the choice had not been hers. Nor, she believed, did Sydney have any say in responding as she had. Their paths had been meant to cross, and so they had. Such were her thoughts as they morphed into memories and then into dreams, deep in the dark of the forest.

Mena was startled from sleep as one vision crossed over and collided with another, culminating in a physical move that had her roll over and illuminate the dial on her watch. It was three in the morning. Since she was already wide-awake, she decided to start the day early. She grabbed her Maglite, quietly unzipped the flap of her tent, and walked out into the woods.

By the light of a nearly full moon, Mena steered her Jeep north, enjoying the crisp, cool air on her face, so unlike what she'd find this time of year at home. Because she hadn't had much, if any, sleep, she turned the radio on to help keep her from nodding off.

Although most of the crew was centered far to the south, in the Red Rock State Park and Stoneman Lake areas, instinct told her to veer north. Maybe as far as Antelope Hill on the western side of her designated turf and toward Humphrey's Peak, the northernmost boundary of the Coconino National Forest. As she headed up Highway 180 out of Flagstaff and turned onto Schultz Pass Road, on what she thought would be a leisurely early morning drive, she was hoping to clear her thoughts. But she was quickly snatched from that fantasy and slowed the Jeep to a crawl. The air, which only moments before had been so refreshingly pure and pristine, was polluted by the unmistakable smell of wood burning.

Pulling over to the side of the road, Mena clicked on her light and checked the maps folded on the passenger seat. Once she'd found the right one and oriented herself to her location, she couldn't believe it! She was miles north of where the fires had started, where the crews were working, in an area they'd checked out, cleared, and considered safe days ago. How could fire this far up have eluded detection? And for how long? She continued onto Forest Road 557, Mt. Elden Lookout Tower Road, where the asphalt gave way to dirt, switchbacks, and hairpin turns. The dust plumes added to the already hazy sky made visibility tough, but she finally had the structure in her sight, or at least she thought so.

"Shit, shit, shit!" She slammed her hand against the steering wheel after realizing she'd mistaken the rise of a nearby radio communications tower for the lookout and taken a wrong turn. With no time to spare, she left her Jeep there, grabbed her binoculars and flashlight off the seat, and scrambled upward through the waist-high undergrowth.

Although the sun would soon rise, the night sky remained dark for the moment, except for a weakening moon's waning light. No stars could be seen above. Whether due to the time of day or the ever-thickening clouds of smoke, Mena couldn't tell and didn't know. Her lungs coughed in protest and her nostrils stung as she slipped on loose dirt and tiny stones, sliding two steps down for every three she took up. She cursed in frustration and forced herself to pick up her heels.

Finally, as she rounded a bend in the trail, the tower came into sight. At only the base of the steel high rise, she still had four sets of metal stairs left to reach the platform above. As she climbed, from her ever-increasing vantage point, she felt the shifting winds pick up and heard the newly energized breeze as it whistled through the tops of the bending trees below, giving way to the northerly flow.

Although the worst of the smoke had yet to reach the peak, there was no mistaking the stronger smell of a burning forest, but where was it coming from? Seeing no evidence the tower's engulfing was imminent, she quickly scrambled to the top.

Once there, she looked around and was amazed by what she saw. Visible to the naked eye, an army of angry, orange flames shook their fists from spots on all sides. In some places, far-reaching tendrils swirled and spiraled on their way from the earth's natural kindling upward, toward the wide expanse of sky.

She turned the small, circular wheel of the high-powered binoculars' lenses to bring the scene into its sharpest focus. Slowly scanning the distance, amidst the haze of blue-green branches, she saw the disaster's source. Sparks and embers raced to break away from a larger swath of burning woodland. Catching airwaves, the embers rode them north like a skilled surfer. Hot spots had jumped the zone, but why so many? Why so fast and so far?

Mena reached for her radio, only to find that in her haste to climb the hill to the tower, she'd forgotten it in her Jeep below.

Frantically, she hurried back down to the ground and ran as fast as she could go. It seemed like it was taking her forever to get back to where she'd started out. She wondered whether it was possible she'd lost her bearings and was headed in the wrong direction when the ground beneath her, as if itself in retreat from the advancing fire, gave way, causing her to lose her footing. She slid, then tumbled headfirst down the steep slope and into the concealing brush, where some unknown object reached up and abruptly stopped her momentum.

LESS THAN TWENTY MINUTES LATER, Mike Davila, the assigned lookout and fire behavior analyst on loan from Missoula, Montana, unknowingly drove past her slackened body lying unconscious nearby, though far off the road. His sense of smell, too, was the first of the five alerted to the surprise that awaited him. He rounded the last bend and parked his truck at the base of the tower. Fearing what he would find, he stopped and radioed in before he even climbed up.

"Base camp. This is Davila reporting from Elden Mountain Lookout Tower, about four miles north of mile marker 16, just to the west of Highway 89. There is definitely something on fire here. I'm going up to check it out. Over."

He'd no sooner reached the top when his mouth fell open in awe.

"I have numerous spots on all sides. I repeat. Numerous spots on all sides."

After calling in the necessary coordinates, so those unfamiliar with the area could plot the site's location, Davila hurried down from the tower and prepared to join the rest of the men who would soon arrive in their efforts to tame the beast breathing fire from all fronts.

As he sat on the bottom step of the lookout, putting on his boots and protective outer gear, the sleepy but slowly rising sun managed to break through the particle-flecked clouds on the horizon and was strong enough to reflect a glint his eyes couldn't readily identify. Davila, always alert and curious by nature, made his way down the other side of the hill through the brush toward the source of the light, and he was surprised for the second time that morning by what he found. The sun had singled out and bounced off either the windshield or a mirror of a Jeep Wrangler that had been parked on the other side of the maintenance road, but there was no one inside nor anywhere around.

He again pushed his two-way button. "Base Camp. Peña, come in. This is Davila again. About one hundred yards to the west of the tower's base, at the bottom of the slope…there's a vehicle here, a Jeep, with no one inside. Over."

ISABEL SALAS, HEARING THIS, NEARLY spilled her hot coffee all over herself as she frantically reached for her mobile unit and responded, "Davila. Come in. It's Isa."

"Davila here."

"Mike, what's the model and color? Over."

"It's a black Wrangler."

Isa's heart skipped a beat as she sent out a silent plea, *Oh my God, no! Please let her be alright.* As the only other woman firefighter on the crew, Mena was a friend.

"I think it might be Mendoza's," Isa said, "which means she must be there somewhere. I'm on my way!"

Plotting the tower's location from ten miles south, Isa, who had been heading in the opposite direction, turned her Civic around on the dusty park road and mumbled a thanks for the maneuverability of small cars. She never did like how pickups fishtailed.

Seeing and pulling in beside Davila's truck, the two met up at the base of the tower, and Mike quickly led her to the Wrangler, which she confirmed as Mendoza's. Clipping her radio to her belt, she started out one way while he went in the opposite direction.

"Mena!" she called repeatedly, receiving no response. All she heard was Davila's voice echoing her shouts. Within minutes, a small ground fire blew up in their vicinity, but it posed no real threat to them and they easily smothered it. However, it served as a brutal reminder that time was of the essence. Fearing several of the spots could join forces, create dangerous conditions, and make it necessary for them to abandon their search, Isa worried and wondered where Mena could be and why she hadn't responded to their calling.

"Why don't you keep searching down here while I head back up the tower for another look?" Mike suggested. "I need to make sure we're safe here and see if I can get an idea for how long. It's not likely, given the density of the surrounding forest, but I want to try and see if I can see anything from up top."

Isa agreed it was worth a shot as she continued calling Mena's name, crisscrossing the area and trying to imagine where she might have gone. The very wind carrying her voice off into the distance blew a little stronger, enough to part the branches of the trees and reveal a tiny spot of unnatural color further west in an area neither had yet searched.

Mike saw her looking up in his direction and pointing toward what had caught her eye.

"I see it too!" Mike radioed Isa before preparing to join her back on the ground.

When she had all but given up hope of finding it, there it was again. A piece of Mena's yellow Nomex shirt. She would never again curse the brightness of the fabric that could be seen from where she was, down in the brush.

"I found her!" Isa radioed. She then instructed Mike, "Hurry! Call 911!"

In no time, Mike reached them and stooped to pick Mena up.

Isa could tell Mena was dead weight in his arms, but at least she wasn't dead! *Perish the thought!*

The bulging veins in Mike's neck, his tight-lipped mouth, and the sound of his breathing let her know that despite his physical fitness, it was a struggle to carry Mena's limp body up the hill. Isa looked at the gash on her head, oozing bright red, yet it was already crusting over with dry, darkened blood. As Mike laid her down on the ground, the rise and fall of Mena's chest showed her breathing was steady but shallow. More worrisome than that was the fact that she was nonresponsive, out cold.

"It looks like she took a nasty fall. Best I can tell, she hit her head on a rock or a tree on the way down. In my truck, there's a water bottle and a first aid kit," Davila said.

Before he'd even asked, Isa was on her way to get them.

He poured water over a piece of gauze and gently dabbed around the wound.

"I didn't want to move her, but I couldn't leave her out there. Who knows how long before help gets here or this whole area goes up?"

"You did the right thing, Mike."

Isa stooped by Mena's side and felt for her pulse. Just as she felt pressure on her wrist, Mena moved her head from side to side and appeared to be waking up.

"Mena. Mena, can you hear me?" Isa asked.

"Syd?" Mena mumbled with closed eyes and a furrowed brow.

"What?" Isa asked. "What did you say? It's me, Isa," she repeated. But Mena's body quickly went slack again as she appeared to slip further into unconsciousness.

Thankfully, a siren could be heard as the rescue vehicle approached from the south. A helicopter, which now circled the area, had been placed on standby, in the event they needed to airlift her. Jumping out of the cab of the transporter, the paramedics grabbed a handheld stretcher from the back, threw an oxygen mask and tank on top, and set out for the tower in a run.

As one checked Mena's blood pressure and pulse, the other pulled out a light and shined it into her eyes, lifting her lids to check her pupils' response. "Any idea how long she's been out?" he asked.

"No, I'm afraid not. I pulled up at about four-twenty and shortly after found her vehicle here. We found her about three quarters of an hour after that, about a hundred yards down that way." Davila pointed.

The EMTs looked at and dressed the open wound on the side of her head near the temple, immobilized her for the journey, then placed her on the stretcher and lifted it.

Isa looked at Mike, then at them, and asked, "Mind if I come along?"

Mena was transported to Flagstaff Medical Center with what was being considered a possible life-threatening head injury. She remained unresponsive and unconscious. In the ER, doctors examined her and nurses hooked her up to an IV and various other bags and monitors as Isa anxiously awaited word on her condition.

It seemed like an eternity had gone by before one of the more compassionate nurses came out with the news that, "It may be a while before she comes around. We're going to move her to the critical care unit, where trained staff can keep watch over her until she does." Isa was told she could wait there, that visits with patients in the CCU were restricted to brief interludes, and that someone would soon be out to give her more information.

About twenty minutes later, another nurse came out of the double doors into the waiting area where Isa sat.

She jumped to her feet when she heard, "Family for Mendoza?" called.

The nurse asked Isa as she approached, "Are you family?"

Isa nodded her head. "We're sisters." Given the circumstances, she didn't see any harm in the lie. After all, they were sisters in a sense—as much members of the sisterhood of firefighters as the men could be brothers.

The nurse led her to Mena's bed, where yet another nurse was by Mena's side, recording her vitals on a chart. She smiled as Isa walked in.

Isa waited for the other one to leave before admitting honestly, "I'm a friend. I was there when she was found."

The nurse smiled in understanding, letting her know rules were sometimes meant to be bent and that she wouldn't tell anyone they were skirting hospital policy.

Isa looked at her name badge—Alexandra Pogue, RN—and said, "Thank you."

Alex smiled, finished up what she was doing, and left the room so Isa could visit in private.

She spent her five minutes looking at Mena, overwhelmed by emotion and silently crying. "Mena," she spoke to her usually strong friend who now looked so helpless in the bed. "Why didn't you tell anyone where you were going? Why do you always have to be so damned independent?" she yelled.

Before she could berate Mena much more, Alex was back. She held a clear plastic bag in her hands, in which Isa could see Mena's uniform and what must have been her personal belongings. "Would you like to sign for this?" she asked Isa. "It's everything that was on her when she was brought in." She handed her the bag, recorded Isa's ID information, then escorted her out and continued with her rounds.

Without breaking the seal at the top, Isa saw a gold chain, a wallet, and some keys inside, on top of the clothes.

She carried it with her back to the waiting area where she sat in a chair and slowly separated the bag's top. In the wallet were twenty-three dollars in cash, an American Express card, Mena's driver's license, and a few business cards. She flipped through them, stopping when a flash of red ink caught her eye. IN CASE OF EMERGENCY CALL had been handwritten down the right edge of one of the cards. Isa pulled it out of its protective liner. It read: Sydney Foster, PhD. Professor of Anthropology and Cultural Studies. University of Maryland. The address was a place called College Park.

Sydney? Syd? Could that have been what Mena had said?

She turned the card over in her hand and went back and forth in her mind, not knowing what to do or whether she'd be jumping the gun if she called the woman. *It's around noon eastern time,* she mentally calculated. *As far as college goes, it's the middle of summer, and odds are there won't be anyone on campus. But dedicated professors usually pick up* messages. With that rationalization, she convinced herself, then stepped out into the hall to dial the number. She was surprised when the phone was answered after ringing only once.

"Sydney Foster," the woman on the other end of the line identified herself.

Isa's mouth went dry as soon as the stranger's voice came on. "Hello, Dr. Foster. My name is Isabel Salas." The silence gave Isa cause to pause and wonder how big of a mistake she'd made in calling. However, not one to be so easily deterred, she forged on. "I'm a friend of Jimena Mendoza."

Sydney's heart skipped a frantic beat, and she nearly dropped the phone. She struggled for composure, having both hoped for this day, for word from Mena, and dreaded its ever coming. Thoughts and speculations intertwined as she waited for what seemed like an eternity for the woman to go on.

"There's been an accident. Mena's been hurt."

God…please, no! Sydney silently mouthed and bowed her head over the papers on her desk, struggling to keep the tears at bay and her emotions bottled tight. *Okay, injured means still alive,* she reasoned. But how, and why, had the woman called her?

"We've worked fire lines together for a while now. I didn't…I don't know if she has any family I should call. I was the one who found her. I was just given her things at the hospital. That's when I went through her wallet trying to find something, and I found your card. That's why I'm calling."

Then she wasn't a lover. Oddly, Sydney felt relief before audibly gasping as she remembered the day she'd written on her card and given it to Mena. It surprised her that she'd kept it, that she'd carried it with her to this day.

"Anyway, other than a few dollars, a credit card, a couple of register receipts, and a driver's license, your business card was the closest to a personal link I found. But if you don't mind my asking, how do you know Mena? Are you family?"

Sydney paused momentarily before responding, "We were once very close. Time and circumstance have since come between us, but I still care for her very much. Thank you for calling."

Not one for dragging out small talk under the best of circumstances, Sydney asked Isa for the name and location of the hospital and told her she'd be there as soon as she could. The phone had barely clicked off before she was back on the line calling Southwest Airlines and a hotel to make reservations.

CHAPTER 2

BACK ON THE FIRE LINE, Peña did his best to stand his ground and send his guys out at the end of their twelve-hour duty days, but that was seldom possible during an initial attack or when conditions warranted the need to have them work longer. And it was tough for other reasons. He knew what it was like to leave before the job was done. He'd been one of them for a long time. It's unthinkable to walk out while a fire rages out of control. For most of them, it was a calling, not a job, and the day didn't follow the hands of a clock. You stayed until you were no longer needed, 'till the work was done, then you went home to a tent in a field or a parking lot until the fire was completely out.

But Peña also knew well-rested men were more alert and less likely to make mistakes. They could do more than just push a shovel and swing a Pulaski; they could put some thought into their actions and move faster. So he insisted they take regular breaks with the threat of permanently cutting the noncompliant from the squad. Thankfully, lots of fresh volunteers were pouring in from all over the country. This fire was making national news, and it had the attention of everyone. Even nature groups that loved this land, like the Sierra Club, would do what they could to save their outdoor home.

Their biggest and most immediate concern now, as they fought fiery flames on all fronts, was being surrounded with no way out. Several times already, they'd had to relocate their incident command post to a new safe zone when the previous one became no longer so. The culprit had been the surface fuels: branches, twigs, cones, and dead vegetation. They couldn't get ahead; they were having enough trouble keeping up.

The intensity of the heat made it feel like those on the line were inside an oven. The heavy protective clothing they wore only served to weigh them down more, slowing them in their race against time, but it was all regulation. If the fire, heat, and smoke weren't enough, there was always plain old exhaustion. That's why paramedics were on hand with plenty of water and tanks of oxygen, which they had to be careful to keep away from the heat. They'd set up their own *M*A*S*H* community on the outskirts of hell town. There, they waited for the weak and weary to come. Before releasing the men back to the blaze of the battleground, they routinely checked blood pressures and for signs of dehydration.

The rangers had heard a rumor that there were more than a dozen fires in the Coconino National Forest alone, ranging in size from one acre to more than a thousand. With strength in numbers, they joined forces to their left and right, growing larger and mightier, refusing to bow in defeat to the enemies who fought to put them out. Small flashy fuels—consisting of dry grass, leaves, pine needles, twigs, and other dead brush—served the fire as highly combustible kindling, but it was the wind that posed the biggest threat. Every time they had the main fire surrounded by cleared lines that had been dug by hand and connected to existing trails, roadways, streams, and rocky areas that served as natural breaks in the terrain, the air would increase its speed and often change direction, defying all their hard-earned accomplishments.

Although the men and women on the ground moved in quickly to mop up hot spots, fledgling fires jumped across previously cleared safe zones, and they were having trouble keeping the phoenix from rising from the ashes over and over, breathing new fires they fought valiantly to fend off. But they kept on, refusing to give up. Side by side and on all fours, they crawled through the hot and smoldering duff. As they moved, puffs of smoke were forced out of the ground by the weight of their bodies as they searched for underground hiding places where fire had buried itself, waiting for a later flare up.

When they came upon an area they had doubts about, the finder would order the line to "Stop!" Using their hands or shovels, the feelers would turn the cooler earth on top over and under in an attempt to smother any subterranean embers, forcing the last dying breath of the fire out. Sometimes water was available, thanks to pumper trucks, and engine crews would drag lines of hose far into the woods, willing and eager to douse. Not until everyone was convinced any chance for re-ignition had been extinguished would they clear the area and continue with their dirty forward march.

"RUN! GET OUT OF HERE!" Peña warned his crew. They'd feared the worst the moment they saw how fast the fire raced behind them up the hill. He called out to the others as loud as he could and hoped they could hear him over the roar of the fire. "To the safety zone! Everyone! Get out of here now!"

The men dropped their tools, some even their packs, and ran as fast as they could. Several followed. Some, in a panic, left others in the wake of their dust.

Isa, back from the hospital and with them, mumbled an out-of-breath prayer as she fell in step, breathing hard and stretching herself to her limits to keep up with their longer strides and quicker paces. "Holy Mary, Mother of God!"

She pulled the rosary out from under her shirt and held the rosewood beads against her mouth. The soles of her boots slapped the hard and relentless earth beneath her feet as she followed the blur of yellow shirts she hoped would lead them out. *Not yet, please, dear God, not now, not here, not like this.* She begged and pleaded for just a little more time. She didn't want to die without having yet really lived, loved, or been loved. She didn't want to die, period! Her heart pounded in her chest, and her lungs ached with every breath and step she took.

"Come on, hurry up!" She heard the guys in front as they encouraged those trailing behind to pick it up. They were so close that if one were to miss a single step, like dominoes, they would all come down. The sound of frightened men and women gasping for oxygen, the smell of fear and sweat, that distinct aroma of imminent death, permeated the fiery air and mixed with the stench of burning sap, grass, and bark.

The group of front-runners rounded a bend and broke apart, some choosing one direction while others went their own ways. Isa imagined they were following primal instincts they hoped would make a difference in a race in which only the fittest would survive. She went as far as she could until it was only her mind still capable of running, after her legs simply gave out.

While the others continued to outrun their fates, she seemed to accept hers for what it was, and with a "Me rindo, Señor," sat to await the coming of the Lord on what she feared would be her grave.

When Peña, who had been directly in front of her, looked back, he saw she was no longer following. "Salas!" he called.

Whether pulled back of their own accord or by that of guilty consciences, the others heard him and stopped in their tracks. As much as they feared for their own lives, they couldn't abandon one of their own, not out here, where she didn't stand a chance alone.

"Go on!" Peña insisted. "Keep going! I'll go back." And with that, he waved them off and turned, retracing his steps toward the far-reaching fingers of the unfurling inferno. He found Isa where she'd fallen, about fifty feet back. Curled up in a fetal position with her arms over her head, she was rocking herself slowly, crying and praying. With no time for communication, he bent over her, picked her up, and ran with her in his arms.

He could hear the beast as it galloped behind them. He felt its breath on the back of his neck. Still he ran, surrounded by the voices of the others. Some were asking their God for forgiveness, others sent out never-to-be-heard messages of *goodbye* and *I love you*, and a select few bargained for the miracle of salvation, offering promises of change and renewal should they make it out alive.

That's when Peña shouted, "This is it, guys! The moment we hoped would never come! It's now or never! The only chance we've got! Deploy your units!" That was the signal for the men to pop open their Shake 'n' Bakes, the emergency blankets they hoped would protect them from the fatal intensity of the heat. But against a fire of this magnitude, they weren't too convinced.

Despite the noise of the fire all around, Peña heard zippers being pulled open and the rustle of canvas pouches as they were emptied, then the crinkle of aluminum fabric unfolding. He stopped and placed a limp Isa on the ground so he could get out his own. Knowing there was no way she could take care of herself, he had no choice but to pull his shelter over them both. He quickly scuffed away the duff with the sole of his boots, moved Isa onto the dirt he'd cleared, and laid his body over hers. While holding the rear of their life preserver down with the toes of his boots, he pulled the front over them like a cocoon and held down the sides as close to the ground as he could. There was nothing else to do.

Beep... beep... beep...

The monitors attached to Mena in her hospital room had sounded steadily for so long that Alex was momentarily stunned to find they had changed their tune. But when Mena began unexpectedly thrashing about, causing alarms to go wild, she hurried into action. Mena's abrupt movements had tangled some of the wires she was hooked up to and knocked others loose, wreaking havoc and speeding up the electronic waves bouncing off the walls and around the room.

At first, Alex's fear was that Mena might be convulsing, but as she moved closer to get a better look, she realized she must have been having a terrifying dream of some sort.

As she untangled and reattached sensors that had twisted and come off, she spoke to Mena softly, soothingly, "Sh... it's okay. You're okay. You're safe here in the hospital."

"No, no!" Mena kept repeating. "Not safe, the fire! I have to help!"

Mena was finally waking up. Alex pulled the rail up on the far side of the bed to keep her from falling, then, in an attempt to calm her, she gently leaned over and touched Mena's shoulder. At the contact, Mena gasped, sat straight up, and reached for her, crying and emitting what sounded like a wounded animal's wailing.

"It was just a dream. It's okay," Alex comforted her.

Mena's breathing finally slowed, and Alex let go.

"It was all so real," Mena said.

"Well, if you feel like telling me what you dreamed about, I might be able to reassure you that's all it was."

"There was a fire." Mena paused as she attempted to recall the details that had frightened her during the night.

"Go on. What else?"

"Isa was there, in the fire. And some of the others. She was hurt. Badly. Well, I don't really know, but my crew had to deploy their shelters, and that's never a good thing."

Compassion showed on Alex's face. "Maybe it'll help you if I tell you that your friend Isa is just fine. She was here earlier, maybe that's why you dreamed of her, but I can assure you she hasn't been hurt. As a matter of fact, no one, other than you, has been brought here from the fire. Thankfully."

Alex kept a close eye on the readings of the monitors that were busy tracking her vitals.

Eventually, Mena exhaled loudly, licked her lips, and leaned back on the pillow Alex had repositioned behind her head. Her eyes were open, but they didn't appear to be completely focused. Alex's attention was divided between what was happening with Mena and the machines, and just as she was about to call for the attending physician, Mena drifted off again. After a few minutes of watching her for any changes in her condition, Alex wrote some notes on her chart and left to report what had happened to the medical team.

MENA'S EYES FLUTTERED, THEN SLOWLY opened, and she started to truly wake up. As she left her protective comatose state behind in the fog, her head pounded. A hypersensitivity to any and all forms of light was the next sensation she became painfully aware of, as the pupils of her eyes alternated between extremes of dilation. She had to learn how to adjust to the intensity of all that was white, bright, and painful to her eyes, shielded as they had been for so long by the dark of sleep. The first face she saw was one that was unrecognizable to her for the moment, but it would soon become quite familiar.

"Well, hello there," Alex greeted her with a smile.

Mena's eyes continued to blink as Alex took her wrist to check her pulse. "We're glad to have you back, Ms. Mendoza."

Mena heard the voice and understood the words, but her eyes were having trouble focusing. With excruciating effort, she managed to keep them mostly open. As she became aware that she was no longer out in the forest, but lying in a hospital bed, Mena gathered the strength and lucidity to ask, "How long have I been here? How long have I been out? What happened?"

"How much do you remember?" Alex asked as she rang the station for attention. When the desk nurse entered, she told her, "Go get Dr. Johnson. This time, our patient really is waking up."

Alex reached for the controls and slowly raised the head of the bed, just a little, enough so Mena could take a sip of water, which would better enable her to talk. She moved the Styrofoam cup closer and bent the flexible straw over and into her mouth. Mena managed to wet her lips, that was all, but it was enough for now.

Too tired to take more, she backed her head away, laid it gently against the pillow, and closed her eyes before she spoke. "I remember the fire, and the smoke, and running to the Jeep for my radio. That's all."

Alex told her, "That's a good start. It will all come back to you in time. For now, while we wait for the doctor, I'll fill in a few of the blanks for you. Two of your fellow firefighters found you. One of them saw an empty vehicle and went in search of its owner. That would be you, so I'm told." She smiled before going on. "From the report I got, you were found somewhere north of the city, near a place called Elden Tower. One of your rescuers, your friend Isa, came with you in the ambulance. She's still here."

Mena looked around.

"She just went down the hall to get a bite to eat. She's going to be upset with me when she gets back. I assured her there was no way you'd wake up during the few minutes I forced her out. But to get back to your original question, only been a few hours since they brought you in."

Mena struggled to sit up, but her head reeled, and the room spun, so she allowed Alex to take her by the arm and gently ease her back down.

"Whoa there, missy! Not so fast. That was quite a fall you took, you know."

Mena remembered her head, and the blood. She reached up and felt the bandage just as the doctor pulled aside the curtain and came around.

"You gave us quite a scare, Ms. Mendoza," he said, "but your friend down the hall had faith in you and knew you'd pull through. And it looks like she knew what she was talking about." He pulled the films and test results out. "I just got the results of your MRI. It looks like whatever swelling that may have caused you to concuss is all but gone now. I see no reason you won't make a full recovery, and it looks to me like you're on your way."

He then turned to Alex and said, "Go ahead and decrease the drip, slowly. We should be able to take her completely off it within the next day or two. If all goes well, as it's showing every indication it will, she should be able to get out of here shortly after that." With that, the doctor said his goodbyes and moved on to the next patient along the route of his rounds.

At that very moment, Isa returned from the cafeteria and entered the room to find Alex by Mena's side.

"Mena," Isa spoke softly, "It's so good to see you awake, to have you back with us."

"She's still having a lot of pain," Alex explained, as she checked the dosage of chemical relief the doctor had ordered. "It's normal. Her body is waking up, and her mind is attempting to process the extent of the damage. Although we're decreasing the amount of medication keeping her sedated to deter movement, we had to give her a stronger dose of another to help ease the pain. She'll go back to sleep or be in a groggy daze, I'm afraid, for a while longer."

Seeing the anxious and pained expression on Isa's face, Alex shared, "The doctor was just here with the results of her scan, and there doesn't appear to be any swelling."

Isa tried her best to smile at the news before the nurse reminded her, "Even so, she's not quite out of the woods yet." She looked at Isa and smiled softly. "You'll want to make sure she takes it easy for a few more days and do your best to keep her from getting involved in anything too physically strenuous or mentally upsetting until she's made a complete recovery."

CHAPTER 3

LATER THAT EVENING, HER BAG packed and her digital boarding pass in hand, Sydney stared into an empty fireplace. The whole house was empty. Even her dog, Jenny, who'd been dropped off with a neighbor, was gone. Numb and still in shock, Sydney settled back in her chair and relived the conversation she'd had with Isa. While savoring the warm and calming effect of the scotch on the rocks, she wondered if she'd missed anything.

It was only by a stroke of luck that she'd been in her office that morning to take the call. With only five days left until the start of the second mini-mester, she'd been unable to focus at home and had gone in to work on a syllabus. She was diligently pounding away at one when the phone rang. Normally, she didn't teach during the summer. Instead, she used the free time to travel, research, and write. For the second year in a row, however, she thought the class and students would serve her as a much-needed distraction. How life can change in an instant!

Steeling her nerves for the rollercoaster that was soon to come, Sydney polished off the near-empty bottle of White Horse and put her plane reservation in her purse before heading upstairs to the bedroom. She had once shared it with Mena, who—thank God—she hadn't lost. Her mind swirled with memories of the time she'd spent with Mena, wondering about all that had happened since she'd last seen her and the imaginings of what she would find now. Not just physical damage that may have been done, but emotional scarring that may have taken its toll. Eventually, her body's need for rest won out over the stress of her mind, and she was able to drift off. But a peaceful sleep was not to be.

She tossed and turned as one dream overlapped and melded into another. During one of her waking moments, between the disturbances created by her subconscious and as she waited for her heart to calm its beating, she decided it was no use and gave up. Reaching for the notebook she kept on her bedside table, she recorded a date and wrote down all that she remembered.

It wasn't the first time she'd dreamed of a tiger, and she wondered again why the animal was so present in her mind. The last time, as she'd watched a young woman she'd been having lunch with walk away and up some concrete steps, the big cat had sauntered across the grass at the top of the hill. As the woman reached the place where their paths would cross, the animal turned to go right down the stairs on the other side of the rail. The woman turned to her right at the top and walked off. This time, there was a storm, and she was at home. Lightning lit the backyard in intervals, and each time, she saw the tiger, getting closer and closer. Just as it crashed through her back patio's door, she woke up.

She'd been intrigued by the meaning, the symbolism inherent in the appearance of such a returning beast, and she looked it up. Most everything she read interpreted the night vision to mean the dreamer was running away from personal feelings and emotions. *I guess they were close to catching up to me this time*, she thought.

She closed her spiral, put her pen away, and thought about her time with Mena, where it had gone wrong. Not wanting to rock the boat too early in their relationship, she hadn't told Mena how she'd felt like she was losing control. It was no longer she alone who decided how each day would unfold; now there was another making choices for her. One with no idea how even a simple act like pocketing the car keys instead of leaving them on the counter was causing her fear and anxiety.

While Sydney had told Mena about her uncle and what he'd done, she hadn't explained to Mena how that translated into her need to feel safe at all times and at all costs. How something as seemingly insignificant as Mena closing a door Sydney had left open when showering had affected her sense of security and caused her panic attacks to return. She had, eventually, brought it all up with a therapist in counseling, and that had worked wonders, but there was much she'd never revealed to Mena. They had really just begun to scratch the surface of one another when their time together was cut short.

BEFORE SHE KNEW IT, IT was six a.m., and although she had barely slept a wink, most people were just rousing themselves for a day at work. After showering and dressing, Sydney loaded her bag into her car and closed the trunk. She headed east on Interstate 70 toward Baltimore-Washington's Thurgood Marshall International Airport. Traffic on the highway was starting to pick up. She'd left earlier than she needed to, concerned she'd run into a stalled rush once she hit Interstate 695, Baltimore's Beltway. It had far too many loops, lanes, entrances, and exit ramps for a driver at her most alert; that was something Sydney, at the moment, was not. She hadn't stopped thinking about Mena since she'd received the call. Since then, even more old memories and what-ifs had clouded her brain, forcing out all other thoughts.

Before she knew it, she was making her way toward the terminal's long-term parking lot. After exiting the empty shuttle, she rolled her bag through the building, catching only a glimpse of the large stained glass crab that stood as an otherwise stately visitor's welcome. The first time she'd met Mena at the airport, they'd posed for a picture in front of the sculpture's giant front claws, a memory that still served as her cell phone's lock screen. This morning, however, she didn't allow herself to linger in the memory for long. She rolled her wheels away from the artfully crafted crustacean before her tears could fall.

She removed her shoes and placed her purse and bag on the conveyor belt that would pull them through the security screening block. Having packed nothing but clothes, there was no reason for scrutiny or delay, thus she was able to quickly move through to the gate at the end of Southwest's hall. There, she joined several other travelers in wait, some businessmen and women, visiting relatives, and other vacationers.

The flight was bound for Phoenix, a desert city steeped in triple-digit heat, deep in the heart of the weather map's blistering red zone. As a die-hard northerner who loved the change of seasons and couldn't live without the refreshing cold and invigorating snow, Sydney couldn't imagine why anyone would choose to live or even go to such an inferno of a place without a compelling reason or for more than a temporary sojourn.

She allowed her thoughts to drift for a moment to the heat she'd suffered during her previous stay. She didn't know how Mena could stand it in southern Arizona. She stopped her memory there before she got too caught up in the depths of emotions in which she could easily drown. Over the years, she had mastered the technique of keeping her feelings far beneath the surface. Now wasn't the time to let the deluge pull her into the undertow. She switched her focus to the purpose of her journey, where it remained, until it was interrupted by a voice over the intercom, announcing her flight's preparation for departure.

Once inside the aircraft, she squeezed her bag into the overhead compartment, plopped in the nearest seat, and buckled up. She wasn't used to flying coach, but it was only going to be a three-and-a-half-hour flight, and she was prepared to make the sacrifice to be on the earliest plane she could find to her destination. Ordinarily, she would have read or slept, but in such cramped quarters and given the circumstance, she knew she'd be able to do neither and that every minute would be agonizingly stretched out.

As the Boeing 737 was pushed away from the gate and taxied down the runway, she closed her eyes and only vaguely heard the flight attendant as she, on behalf of the captain, welcomed them aboard Flight 1858 with nonstop service to Phoenix, Arizona before going over the safety procedures. Soon after, the jet took off.

ISA WAS IN THE WAITING room by the nurse's station when the entrance door to the building *swished* open and a woman pulling a suitcase on wheels hurried in. She knew, before she'd heard her say, that this was

Dr. Sydney Foster, Mendoza's ex, the woman she'd called. What she didn't know was whether she should approach her and introduce herself or stay back in the shadows and see how Mena's past, in her present and future, would play out.

The nurse at the desk looked up. "May I help you?"

"Yes. Thank you. I'm looking for a patient by the name of Jimena Mendoza. She was brought in yesterday. From the fire, I've been told."

As the woman reached for the patient's file, she asked, "And you would be?"

"I beg your pardon?"

"I'm sorry, but I'm afraid I can't give out any information until a relationship between the visitor and patient has been established. It's hospital policy."

Sydney glared at her incredulously. "I've come from across the country because I was called. I'm listed as her emergency contact. We're…a couple…partners. We're in a relationship."

The desk nurse excused herself and was on her way to check with a supervisor when Alex, who happened to be within sight and earshot not twenty feet down the hall, stopped her and asked, "Erika, what's the problem?"

"The woman at the desk is here to see Ms. Mendoza. Says she's her partner, or something like that."

At that, Alex looked up. Confusion registered on her face, and Isa watched as the bewildered expression gave way to professionalism as she headed Sydney's way.

"Hello, I'm Alexandra Pogue, head nurse on duty. How can I be of help?"

"Thank you, Ms. Pogue. I'm Sydney Foster. Yesterday afternoon, I received a call informing me that Jimena Mendoza was here in this hospital. I've just flown across the country to see her. I got here as soon as I could. As you can see," she said as she motioned toward the bag at her feet, "I didn't even stop at the hotel. I'd like to see her. How is she?"

Erika, back at the desk, went over Mendoza's chart and saw that there was, indeed, a Sydney Foster listed as an emergency contact, as noted by the charge nurse when she'd been brought in. She carried the file over to Alex and apologized to both women for having missed it before. Alex then informed Sydney that Mena was there, being cared for in the critical care unit. She also explained that, due to the serious nature of her condition, she was only allowed one visitor per hour, for a maximum five-minute duration.

"I understand," Sydney much more calmly responded.

Alex ushered her to a chair near where Isa was seated. "I'll come for you when you can see her. Why don't you let me take that for you?" she asked, then reached out for the handle of her luggage.

"Thank you, and please forgive me for being so short-tempered and unmannerly. Not that it's an excuse, but I've been worried sick since I got the call."

Alex smiled at her and excused herself from the waiting area.

From the other side of the room, Isa pretended not to have heard a thing, choosing, for the time being, to remain anonymous.

ABOUT A HALF-HOUR LATER, ALEX returned. "Ms. Foster, you can see Ms. Mendoza now. Come with me," she said as she walked back toward the direction from which she'd come. Pausing only long enough to give medication information to one of the staff, she hit a silver square on the wall, which opened two doors inward, allowing them entry into a large open unit filled with hospital equipment. Some beds were occupied, some were not.

As they walked the length of the room, Alex pointed in the direction of the last one. "She remains stable but unconscious. Of course, that's mostly because of us and the medication she's being given," Alex said as she pulled the curtain back enough to create the semblance of a makeshift doorway.

Sydney took a deep breath, and then she stepped in.

It was there, at that precise moment, amidst the blinding light of overhead fluorescents and the constant cacophony of beeping monitors, that she saw Mena's face and was hit by a wave of emotion. The past and present came together in a rush. Looking at her now, it was as if the clock had remained still, the hands never having reached the fateful day when she made that foolish decision with the consequences of extreme regret and loneliness. But the opportunity she was given to reroute her destiny was not being granted without repercussions. Mena had been seriously injured. The cuts and bruises that covered her body testified to the truth that time had marched on, that now it was her clock that might stop. Sydney stifled a sob and tried not to lose her composure. With her hand over her mouth, she looked silently at the woman lying on the bed before her. Mena's head was wrapped in gauze, and various parts of her body were attached to wires, tubes, and monitors that checked her vitals and pumped medication and oxygen.

Sydney stood for what seemed like an exceedingly long time, just looking at Mena, remembering, reliving, and praying that this would not be how or where she'd again lose her, without hope for a different outcome.

"Oh, Mena," she whispered quietly. "Please come back to me. I need you so." She spoke freely words that before, when they were together, had been so difficult for her to voice.

Unfortunately, Mena was not in a place from which she could now respond, nor had she even heard, but there was one witness to Sydney's words. Alex had either reentered or remained behind her and now stood at the weeping woman's back. She gently touched Sydney on the elbow and handed her a box of tissues before leaving the two of them alone.

Although there was much in Sydney's breaking heart, Mena's name, repeated over and over again, was all that could find its way out of her mouth. Sydney hoped somehow Mena would sense the torrent of emotions that surrounded them, the intensity that had once bound them to one another, and wake up.

Her memory of the first day they'd met was shattered by Alex's return. The reunion that had been so longed for was so short-lived. "I'm sorry, Ms. Foster. I'm afraid time's up. I'm going to have to ask you to leave. As I mentioned earlier, we can only allow visitors for five minutes every hour in the critical care unit. It's best for the patient, and it's needed for her recovery."

"But what if she wakes up or her condition worsens while I'm gone?"

Alex, accustomed to the reactions of loved ones, the fears, the emotions that were so raw, had little more to offer than her word. "I'll come for you as soon as you can see her again. Until then, we'll be watching over her, and we'll let you know the moment there's any change in her condition. I promise."

Having no choice nor say in the matter, Sydney returned to the waiting room.

ONCE SHE'D RESETTLED INTO THE chair in the corner, as far as she could get from the light and noise of the television, Isa took a good look at her. She was an attractive woman, there was no denying that. Well-put-together, in a skirt and blouse with accessories to match. Stylishly dressed, with expertly applied makeup and expensive jewelry. Even her nails had been recently done, the tips painted white in a French manicure; sophisticated, ultra-feminine, maybe even prudish, definitely intellectual. *Okay, maybe some of my observations are being tainted by petty jealousy.* Isa imagined her to be somewhere in her mid-to-late forties, possibly a little older, though she obviously took good care of herself. She was fit and still in shape. But Sydney gave off an air that was so impenetrable and cold. Isa felt the arctic blast from across the room. She wondered how the two of them had ever come to be, let alone been together, as a couple.

Isa was so lost in her wandering thoughts that she hadn't noticed that she was caught gawking. She smiled and walked across the room toward Sydney.

"Dr. Foster?" she asked, as if she didn't already know what the answer was.

"Yes, and I take it you're Isa." It was more of a statement than a question, thus Isa merely nodded her head and sat next to Sydney. "Please forgive me if I seem less than cordial. Quite frankly, I'm afraid I'm still in a bit of shock. Hearing the news with your call, and now, here, seeing Mena. It's just all coming together so fast." A single tear made its way down her face as Sydney's lip quivered, and she worried and twisted a damp tissue in her hand.

In an effort to change the subject, Isa asked, "Have you found a place to stay?"

"Yes, I just didn't take the time to stop at the hotel. In no shape to drive myself. I took a taxi from the airport."

"All the way from Phoenix?" Isa asked, having seen the luggage tag, incredulous at the notion. *This woman is either loaded or loca!* She rebounded from the thought.

"Yes. I thought it best at the time, or maybe I really wasn't even thinking at all. Anyway, depending on how it goes, I can always rent a car locally, should I find I need one."

From there, the conversation veered to details of the accident, and Isa told her as much as she knew. Then, out of curiosity, and because the silence was so thick it was stifling, Isa dared to probe a little deeper. "If you don't mind my asking, how did you and Mena meet? What's your story?"

With the touch of a smile and moist eyes, Sydney answered, "We met in a rather serendipitous way, I guess you could say, after Mena'd read one of the novels I'd written and emailed me to tell me her thoughts about it. I wrote back. Before long, our communication took a more personal turn."

Isa's face lit up, and she scooted forward in her seat, leaning in with interest.

"Soon after, we moved our conversations to the telephone. We spent hours each night talking about everything and nothing at all, if you can imagine. A few months passed before we finally met in person. She surprised me by traveling to California, when I was at a conference. After that, we visited one another regularly and often, until Mena decided it was time to do away with the distance between us by moving across the country."

Isa focused her gaze, smiled, and raised her eyebrows. "How long were the two of you together?"

"That depends on when you start counting." Sydney lowered her head and smiled sweetly, yet sadly. "I'm assuming you want to know how long we lived together, in which case my answer would be a different one. Not quite a year."

With raised and curved brows, Isa asked, "And how long ago did your relationship end?"

Sydney narrowed her eyes before responding. "Mena moved back here, to Arizona, a year ago last winter."

Isa's jaw gaped. She couldn't believe it! *It had been that long!* And this was the woman Mena still held in her heart? *Wow!* She hoped to someday experience that kind of love. But then, what did *she* know? There had to be some compelling reason they were no longer together, and maybe Mena's reluctance to get involved with anyone now had more to do with herself. Maybe she just hadn't cleaned out her wallet in a while. Time would tell, if she couldn't get it out of Sydney first.

"Have you eaten? I was thinking about heading to the cafeteria before our next five minutes with Mena. Would you like to join me?"

"I'd love to."

"Great." Isa stood to lead the way. "It'll give us a chance to get to know each other a little better."

"I'd really like that. After all, you're the only one who can possibly fill in the blanks for me that exist between our then and Mena's now. I've often wondered how she was, what she was doing, where we'd gone so terribly wrong. Maybe you can help me figure it all out." Sydney looked at her with a glimmer of hope in what Isa registered as thawing ice-queen eyes.

OVER A TURKEY SANDWICH AND bottle of cranberry juice, Sydney listened as Isa told her all she knew about her former partner and lover.

"The truth is, I'm afraid I won't be able to provide too many pieces of the puzzle you're hoping to put together. All I really know is that Mena lives alone in Yuma, that she teaches when she's not fighting fires, and that she plays the guitar."

Sydney looked down at the table and smiled.

"What? What is it?"

"Nothing. It's nothing."

"Oh, come on now. There's no way I'm gonna let you get away with not telling me what it is you're thinking. What just turned that sad and worried frown completely upside down?"

"I was just remembering Mena's instrumental inclination, the first time she serenaded me. She had a beautiful voice, so soft, just a little deep. Her words came from a heart that felt so much. She'd given me a beautiful rose and sang me a Spanish song, 'Amar y Querer.' You might know it."

"I do. It's a classic, romantic Mexican ballad."

"Anyway, afterward, we discussed and debated the differences in the language's two similar, yet extremely disparate words for 'love'. In the end, it all came down to semantics, and the emotion Mena had put into her words that day described each indisputably with feelings that would forever live on in my heart and move me in my memory and soul."

"That's absolutely beautiful."

"Yes, it was."

"No, I mean what you shared. It's as if I could see what you must have felt, then and now. Obviously, you have, or had, a very deep and personal connection to Mena. And I must admit, I'm not only a little jealous, but I'm concerned about how Mena's going to react when she finds you here."

Sydney looked at her as if for an explanation.

"I can only imagine the shock and torment such powerful emotions might unleash, and I'm worried Mena might not be in the best place to handle them. What should we do?"

How could Sydney tell her when she didn't know herself?

CHAPTER 4

THE SOUND OF CHAIN SAWS ripping through heavy-boughed evergreens revved, whirred, and roared all around. Nearby, the flames of hot spots seemed to tease, taunt, and laugh at the men, women, and machines failing to keep them from rising. Like reenergized firebirds from the ashes, they jumped over their heads, and—with *whooshes*—ignited more outstretched limbs with their undying sparks.

Peña had to shout to be heard over the *thump-a-thump-a-thump* of helicopter blades from above. The helitack crews within the choppers had been trained to rappel out once they hovered over the right spot.

Other aircraft, including small scooper planes with tanks of retardant and larger heavy-lift helicopters were used to carry siphoned water from reservoirs, lakes, and rivers to where it was needed and was dropped.

Using the arm of his sleeve to wipe the sweat from his face, Peña stopped to hydrate himself for a respite from the unbearable heat and radioed, "Johnson, Becker, Gonzalez, come in."

"Becker here. Johnson, Gonzalez, and Williams are with me. Over."

From his location, about a mile south of Elden Tower, Crew Chief Peña had a responsibility to the men he led on this mission to bring this fire under control. He couldn't afford another injury and needed to know what was going on and where each of his fighters was. "How's it looking where you are?"

"Like a goddamned firestorm! I've never seen anything like it, chief. There are trees burning everywhere I turn, and the smoke is doing its best to drive us out, but into what? God only knows."

Peña made the split-second decision to pull them out. "I need your crew to move west. It looks like several of the larger spots are about to converge, and we need to try to head them off. Stand by for the coordinates." As he waited to be handed the numbers, he reminded Becker, "Don't forget where you are in relation to your anchor point."

Becker was a seasoned fire veteran and, as such, Peña knew he was preaching to the choir, but he also knew emotions ran high in the thick of their work. In the frantic panic and confusion, a man could lose his bearings and forget which direction he was going. Especially when he was running for his life with over a thousand degrees licking hot on his heels with a fiery tongue.

Once latitudes and longitudes were relayed, Peña signed off and ran a hand over the canvas pack attached to his belt. Each of the firefighters had one. It held their only hope for salvation should the fire rage toward them out of control. Other than Peña, Henderson was the most experienced of the crew. He spoke words no one wanted to hear. "We're wasting our time. I've been on the front line lots of times fighting fires like this one. There's too much fuel. There's no way we can stop it. I think we should just all pull out and let it burn."

All around him, frustration mounted. "Then why are you here?" an angry Peña challenged. "You know we don't stop till the fire is out. There are people out there depending on us to save their lives, their homes, this land that they love. Besides, it's racing northwest toward the thick of the woods. If it makes it that far, we're all screwed. We'll be surrounded with no way out!"

That reality silenced them all.

Robles, one of the volunteers who had just joined the squad, asked, "Has the area been evacuated?"

"We've tried, but you know how stubborn some of these homeowners can be," Henderson responded. "We've lost several crews to housing perimeters and wasted water dousing rooftops. They're fighting a lost cause. Residents who choose to build and live nestled away in these forests don't understand the force of an angry nature until it's too late.

There's no way they're not going down. Or, maybe I should say, up in flames. It's not possible for us to save them all."

Peña shook his head and trudged on. Picking up his radio, he pushed the talk button down. "Davila, do you copy?"

The radio crackled for what seemed like too long. Anxiety was high. Then the man's voice came on the line. "Davila here. Over."

"Any word on Mendoza's condition?"

There was no denying her accident had taken a toll on them all. It was the first time any of them had been injured on the line. And even though it had happened before the fire really got going, and it involved a fall rather than a burn or smoke inhalation, it gave them all reason to pause. Made them think about the risks they took, about their own mortality. It brought the possibility of what could happen home. They could try to tame and control it, but fire was a living, breathing being. Given the right amount of oxygen and nourishment, they would never beat it; they could only hope to control it by depriving it of food and air, weakening and squeezing the life out of it. Until then, and as long as it had what it needed, it was and would continue to be a volatile, unpredictable force.

"Last I heard from Salas, she was still down for the count," he came back.

Not knowing how to respond, Peña simply signed off with, "Copy that," and put the radio back on his belt. *Maybe her fall was a blessing in disguise,* he thought to himself. *At least it got her out of this mess.* He immediately felt bad for thinking such a thing. After all, there was no guarantee she'd come out of it any better off than the rest of them. She'd taken quite a fall and had been in and out for a while now.

While fighting fire was their life, blood, and passion, what many of them were born to do, they didn't want to die for it. No one looked forward to getting into the ring with an opponent that outweighed and outboxed them, against whom they didn't stand a chance of winning a round. Meanwhile, Peña and Castillo were doing their best to plot strategies and coordinates on maps, redirect their men, and monitor and record conditions to stave the beast off.

Peña took a good look at his second in command. Castillo was clearly exhausted. They all were. Sweaty and dirty, none of them had stopped to bathe or even put on clean clothes since they got there, and the fire was just heating up. At this rate, there was no way they'd be able to rest and rotate out for a while. Not that any of them would be lined up, waiting to go, no matter how tired they were or how bad things got. Like weary bull riders with no hope of winning a buckle at a rodeo, they'd reached a point where they just wanted to hang on till the buzzer went off, so they could say they had given it their all. But more than twelve hours a day with no real sign of progress had them all feeling down and out.

Still, they forged on. As they did, they recognized the area they were entering oddly bore little resemblance to the one where they'd started out, whether they were in the eye of the storm or this was the calm before what was to come. Either way, they were soon bound to be where the action was. Had they had more time and space, they would have likely brought in bulldozers to do the job.

Alas, Mother Nature waits for no one. Thus, with Reinharts and Pulaskis in hand, they got to work clearing brush, grass, and combustible debris from the dry and hardened ground. Soon after, they were joined by sawyers. Like proud cowboys, they saddled up and sunk three-inch-long metal spikes from their boots deep into the trees' sides and climbed up. Their goal was to bring the biggest young timber down. The job of their sidekicks, the swampers, was to clear away their trimmings, tossings, and cuts, lest they defeat the purpose of the crew's endeavors and serve as a prime tinderbox.

With such a combined effort, it wasn't long before they'd done their job.

Peña's radio went off as Becker reported in, "Base Camp. Come in."

"Peña here. Over."

"Joe. We've done all we can do here. Where to next?"

"I think you boys have earned some time off. Make your way back to the field kitchen and call it a day. We'll see you bright and early in the morning. Over."

THAT EVENING'S MEAL CONSISTED OF rib-sticking, greasy fried chicken, mac and cheese, and green beans. The food was as comfortable as it comes. With Peña busy back at base and Davila still on the frontlines of the fire, it was Henderson who, after grabbing a bite to eat and cleaning up, slipped out to check on Mendoza himself. He was sitting next to her bed in a chair when Salas walked in.

He didn't hear or see her, but she heard him as he whispered, "Mendoza, dammit! Why the hell don't you just wake up? We need you out there. I don't know if I'd say this if I thought there was any chance you'd hear me—hell, your head's already big enough—but you're one hell of a firefighter. You can't quit. You can't give up. You're one of the best we've got. All those times I gave you shit and did my damnedest to piss you off, I was just trying to see what you were made of." He struggled, his voice betraying him by breaking up.

Salas moved back into the shadows and cleared her throat, as if announcing she'd just entered the room, giving the man a chance to dry his eyes and keep his soft side unknown to all but himself.

Henderson stood, moved away from his chair and the bed, and said, "Hey, Salas. I just dropped by to see how Mendoza was. Has she been awake at all?"

"In and out, off and on. Not much. The doctors say they're concerned about pressure building on her brain, so they're keeping her pretty doped up. When they're sure she's out of danger, they'll lessen the meds they're giving her, but until then, what you see is what we'll get. She took a pretty nasty fall." She stopped speaking and looked at Mena.

An uncomfortable silence drifted into the room and wrapped itself around the two of them until Henderson said, "Well, I guess I better get back out there with the rest of the guys."

His words pulled Isa back to the reality of the rest of the crew's situation. "How bad is it?" she asked.

"It's bad. We've got men jumping out of planes and helicopters, coming in from every which way on the ground. They're dumping chemicals and water and doing everything they can. Hell, Boise's even sent down three more crews that had been on another fire up in Montana. If we don't get this thing under control soon, there'll be no stopping it."

"I feel bad, like I should be out there too."

"You're where you're needed right now. If it'll make you feel better, I can have an official order for bedside duty sent down from above." He stood and moved toward the door, but before leaving joked, "Besides, someone's gotta be here when Sleeping Beauty finally decides to wake up." With that, he smiled and walked out the door.

So the man had a heart, of some sort, after all, Salas thought.

She moved to sit in the chair where Henderson had been and looked closely at Mena. Her breathing appeared regular; no alarms, bells, or whistles were going off. She looked like she was simply sleeping. Which, in essence, she was.

Just then, a familiar face came into the room. Alex smiled at Isa and picked up Mena's chart.

"Is it normal for her to still be unconscious?" Isa asked.

Alex finished writing, closed the chart, and looked at her a few seconds before responding. "Let me see if I can explain what's happening with your friend. As you know, when you found her, she was just coming around from having been out for a brief period, we're assuming knocked unconscious. At that time, her brain responded to injury by briefly shutting down. Think of it as what we do with the help of drugs when we put the body into an induced coma for surgery or some other invasive procedure. Because the body wouldn't be able to bear the pain, and might otherwise react violently, we put it to sleep and then wait for it to wake up. Although in Mena's case, initially it was her own body that took on the role of physician and pumped similar natural chemicals into her system to induce the same sleep-like response. We simply picked up where it left off," Alex continued. "We did so because we need to make sure there is no swelling or pressure on her brain. We need to keep her from moving until the full extent of the injury to her head is known. The doctor has already cut back on the medication, so once the IV is removed and she's completely taken off the heavy-duty stuff, she should simply wake up and stay alert, just like we all do after anesthesia wears off."

Alex smiled at Isa, hoping she hadn't seemed too condescending with her simplification, then looked at Mena. "But I don't see any sign of that happening in the immediate future, so why don't you take a break and leave this place for a little while? Take a walk outside. Get a little fresh air and sun. I'll take good care of her while you're gone, and I promise to find you if there's any change in her condition."

THAT CHANGE CAME SOONER THAN expected, and the next time Mena opened her eyes, she stayed awake for more than a few minutes, a fact that was quietly celebrated by all the medical staff who knew her story and had tended to her during her stay.

Mena felt much better than she had the other times she'd rejoined the living for brief interludes. This time, she felt present as she listened to the voices of visitors as they came and went through surrounding rooms. She awaited the regular routine of poking and joking from the hospital staff she'd grown accustomed to spending time with and donating blood to, but nothing could have prepared her for the jolt she received when she saw who followed Isa through the door.

Rendered speechless, Mena thought surely, she must still be asleep and dreaming. She reached for the control to move her bed into a more upright position and swallowed with difficulty. Although she'd hoped and prayed she would one day see Sydney again, she hadn't ever expected to. Yet here she was, at the foot of her bed. *Or was it an apparition, a mere hallucination, a side effect of the drugs? In all their* time apart, she'd had so many conversations with her in her head, but none of those well-planned words found their way anywhere near her mouth now. She simply couldn't believe it, or who she saw.

Shrouded by the intensity of the sustained silence in the room, Isa excused herself by mumbling, "I'm just gonna…I'll be back. See you guys later. Uh, yeah," before turning around and disappearing into the hallway.

Mena and Sydney, alone in the room, silently looked at one another.

Finally, Mena spoke. "Well, now I know how close to death I must have really come." She raised her eyebrows and, with her trademark crooked smile that revealed those deep dimples Sydney had always loved, asked, "But how did you know?"

Sydney nodded her head in Isa's departing direction. "I'm here because your friend, Ms. Salas, called me to let me know what happened."

Mena's forehead creased as she wondered aloud, "How did *she* know? About us? About *you*? I've never told anyone."

Sydney eased into a smile. "That's one mystery I think I can solve. It seems that in all this time, you hadn't removed my card from your wallet. Do you remember? The one I gave you on which I'd written—"

"In case of emergency, call," Mena finished. "Yes, I remember."

The silence between them returned and settled in, as if preparing to stay a while.

This time, it was Sydney who broke the quiet stillness. "For a long time, Mena, I've wanted to talk to you about what happened between us. To explain to you, to try to make you understand why I did what I did." Sydney was not one to easily share details of her personal life or self, especially in such a public space into which anyone could walk and interrupt such an intimate sharing. Yet, realizing this could certainly be her swan song, her final curtain call, her last and only chance for reconciliation…Sydney swallowed her pride and rallied resilience. "It was all too fast, so overwhelming, and different. You came into my life and turned my world upside down. Not that it was a bad thing. I just wasn't prepared for it, for you. I didn't have time to adjust."

Mena didn't know how to respond, so she remained quiet, listening.

"THERE'S SO MUCH I NEVER told you." Sydney pulled a chair closer to the bed. This would take a while, and she didn't want to leave anything unsaid this time around.

 CHAPTER 5

THREE YEARS EARLIER.

Sydney approached the lectern, her reading glasses in hand. Looking over the audience, she took a drink from the glass of water she'd been provided and scanned the crowd. She had accepted the invitation to speak, concerned only a handful of faculty would be interested in what she had to say and that students, even with the bribe of extra credit, would not show up. Thankfully, she had been wrong. Surprised and pleased at the number in attendance for her talk, she relaxed, removed the microphone from its stand, and walked across the stage.

"I'd like to thank you all for taking the time to join me on this lovely afternoon."

She paused to sip more water, giving the hum of the crowd a chance to settle and herself the time to take in the faces that had come.

"I'm not sure I'd have done the same in your places," she went on.

The hall reverberated with the murmur of appreciative mumbles and laughter. After all, it had been a beautiful Saturday.

As a visiting lecturer from the University of Maryland, Sydney had been invited to speak at San Diego State after publishing a well-received scholarly essay on Southern California's neighboring Yuman tribe from the state of Arizona. The host professor, in an attempt to win the support of monies and endowments needed to boost her fledgling department off the ground, had all but pleaded that she come. Ultimately, it was Sydney's own innate interest in indigenous peoples and cultures, coupled with her erudite ego, that had brought her to where she stood on that day. It was there she felt in her element, where she, at that moment, needed to be and belonged.

She spoke at length to the enraptured and gracious crowd of the practices, beliefs, superstitions, and legends of the inhabitants of the Red Rock Canyons and caves on both sides of the lower Colorado River, from Pima Butte across the Trigo Wilderness region and into the Maricopa and Painted Rock Mountains. All were sacred areas to where many in the region still went to get in touch with the spirits of their ancestors, sages who were said to induce dreams to offer guidance and understanding during times of difficulty and trouble.

Sydney soon found herself, as she often did, caught up in the sharing of her research. Perhaps that could explain why, as she neared the end of her talk and the floor was opened to questions, she drifted mentally away in response, almost as if answering without giving the questions much thought. That is, until a rather attractive woman with straight black hair that fell over dark, brooding, and intelligent eyes captivated her with a sonorous voice that demanded attention; the timbre of it was so forceful and strong.

"Tell me, Dr. Foster," the woman addressed her almost intimately from out of the crowd near the front. She stood and looked the speaker in the eyes with a penetrating gaze Sydney sensed could see through to her very soul. "You've obviously spent a great deal of time and effort studying the Quechan. I'm curious to know what it is about them, their history or ways, that has passionately captivated and inspired you to devote so much energy to the exploration of such a relatively small and largely unknown group of people, and so far from your home?"

Sydney was rendered speechless for what, to her, seemed like endless moments, absorbing the burgeoning awareness that this woman was more than just a pretty face in the crowd. Her curiosity not the only sentiment aroused; Sydney floundered for another few moments before clearing her constricted airways. She attempted to regain her usually very calm and collected composure while carefully contemplating the woman whose words and being had challenged and moved her so.

She reached down for the water she'd placed on a shelf of the podium, then looked up, and their eyes locked.

"The Yumans, or Quechans, as you have pointed out by referencing that they were also widely known, among other beliefs, gave importance to the meaning of dreams. It piques my personal interest, especially the value they placed on somnolent symbolism and interpretation."

Sydney hoped no one else noticed her mental fumbling and crumbling.

"It's a well-documented fact," she went on in what was to her perfectionist ears almost a disjointed rambling of sorts, "that the Yumans…Quechans…were fond of using jimsonweed root, both internally and externally as a—"

"I'm more interested in knowing what it is about their beliefs that speaks to you personally, about your dreams, maybe? Have you had visions during sleep? Any that have come true?" She smiled, and the audience chuckled. "For instance, I can tell you that I've had a few, and without any herbal stimulant to help them surface from my subconscious." The crowd made even more noise at that revelation. "What was it, or is it, that has attracted you to this culture so?"

Their eyes remained on one another, again locked. Her inquisitor settled back into her seat, Sydney again paused, and a deafening hush came over the entire auditorium as each listener breathlessly awaited her response.

Who is this woman? Sydney wondered. Never had anyone ever addressed her so casually and candidly. A well-known, highly regarded, and respected scholar in her field, she was accustomed to the questioning of seasoned colleagues and academics who never accepted anything at face value. Much less were they interested in any personal or emotional involvement. Well, apart from one tenured old codger who'd tried to philosophize his way into her bed one whiskey-enhanced debauchery of a night. This, however, was a vastly different, seemingly personal inquiry. Or was she merely reading between unwritten lines? Had she allowed her thoughts to be so distracted, go that out of focus?

Sydney dared look at her. The woman smiled, pleased with herself. No, this woman had no interest in facts and figures. These she appeared to already know. She was after something more, but what? As she struggled to respond, Sydney felt what she feared was the heat of a visible blush.

"Well, I, personally, believe wholeheartedly in the meanings and messages, the symbolism inherent in our dreams. Dear Sigmund… Although he had his faults, and there were many, he was definitely onto something with his id, ego, and superego psychoanalytical explanations, as well as his metaphoric iceberg allusion." The audience rippled once again with muted laughter, and Sydney managed to fall into the rhythm, allowing the camaraderie to relax her enough to break out of the unfamiliar and uncomfortable box into which she'd slid and refocus her thoughts. "Quite honestly, I'm fascinated by the complex capacities and many mysteries of the human mind. And although this is one of my absolute favorite topics of conversation, I'm afraid we're out of time, and I really don't want to wear out my first welcome." She smiled and winked at the woman, abruptly signaling the end of their discussion.

The faculty head made her way to the center of the stage, and so commenced applause.

"Thank you, thank you so very much, Dr. Foster, for such a lively, enlightening, and engaging talk."

AFTERWARD, AT A RECEPTION IN the lobby, Sydney sensed the woman who had shaken the very foundation of her being quietly approach long before her eyes saw her. Her palms began to sweat, and her heart rate picked up.

"I didn't mean to distract you from the intent of your lecture, Dr. Foster," the woman said. "Please accept my apology. But when I found out that you'd be speaking in the area, I couldn't think of a better opportunity, or pass up the chance to help our paths cross." The woman extended her hand in greeting. As if in response to an unasked question, she introduced herself. "I'm Jimena Mendoza."

Sydney nearly dropped the plate and glass she held in her hands. She was literally and figuratively astounded. So this was the mystery woman with whom she'd been exchanging emails for months. And she'd come all the way from Arizona to meet her.

From that fateful moment, their relationship, like a wildfire, ignited and took off. Fueled by engaging discussions and delightful debates, a shared and appreciated intelligence, and an insatiable mental, emotional, and physical appetite, it burned intensely. First via email and snail mail, necessitated by the geographical chasm that separated them by more than two thousand miles. Then by phone, until, unable to withstand the unbearable absences between interludes of in-person intimacies, and the physical back-and-forths, they closed the gap, once, if not for all.

THE HONEYMOON PHASE OF THEIR early togetherness was filled with travels, both to and from their respective homes and to vacation destinations near and far. One of their most memorable journeys was to the Hawaiian Islands.

"C'mon," Mena pleaded and cajoled, "there are so many beautiful fish down in the coral. You can't see or appreciate them from the boat. The water's not as deep over by the rocks, and it's no fun going and seeing them alone."

Sydney, unable to swim and so afraid of drowning, panicked at the thought of having even just her face underwater and balked at putting the mask and fins on.

"I promise I won't let anything happen to you," Mena said. "Trust me. If you don't want to use the vest or float belt, they have a paddleboard with a viewing window you can lay on and see through. I'll pull you around."

Whether because of the splendor of the sun, the joy of the moment, or some other reason yet undefined, Sydney gave in and gave Mena her hand, allowing her to guide her to the steps at the rear of the catamaran.

They were on a charter cruise to the sunken crater of Molokini off the coast of Maui at the time. Sydney had managed to be firm with her refusal to snorkel at both Black Rock and at the resort where they were staying on the Ka'anapali coast. But the beauty of the day and fervent desire of her lover conspired to help her shed her fear and inhibitions as she donned her light blue tankini top, swim shorts, wide-brimmed sun hat, and slathered on the Kōkua Sun Care. Soon, she was pointing out tangs and Picasso fish, and wincing away from eels herself. At her first sighting of the humuhumunukunukuapua'a, Hawaii's state fish, she was giddy with the excitement of a child.

THE FIRST TIME THEY'D MADE love, Mena was the one to chart their course. They'd gone hiking near the Shenandoah River at Harper's Ferry in West Virginia. The afternoon had been a beautiful autumn one. When they'd tired of trekking the trails, they made their way through the historic town, their day outdoors culminating in a climb up to Jefferson Rock. From that vantage point, they could look out over three states: Maryland, Virginia, and West Virginia. It was no wonder the area was considered strategic during the nation's civil war.

After resting there for a while, enjoying the view, the cool breeze, and the warm sun, they went in search of a few sandwiches and found a place under a colorful maple tree that still held onto many of its leaves; they were no longer green, now varying shades of red, gold, and brown. Mena and Sydney spread out a blanket they'd packed in the trunk of the car and relaxed before beginning the short ride home.

Mena couldn't remember ever having felt so much happiness, enjoyed anyone's company more, believed so strongly in the possibility of love. Sydney had already reached and touched a place deep inside her where no one had ever gone. They'd spent countless hours together talking about so many things. Sitting across from one another on the bank of the peaceful river that day, they'd even enjoyed saying nothing at all.

After they finished eating, they stretched out across the grass and allowed a glass of wine they'd brought along to induce the heat of a blush. They felt comfortable in each other's company and arms, so much so that Mena allowed impulse to take control. Leaning slowly forward, closer and closer, unsure, she gave Sydney the chance to stop what she surely knew was coming. Sensing no more hesitation than that of a desire on the verge of being explored, Mena's lips brushed Sydney's lightly. She pulled back, then inclined her head and moved a little closer, then a little more.

Their mouths met in a sweet mingling of emotion that intensified with each tender caress and touch. Their eyes searched deep into each other's soul. Reaching out to one another, hands moved and warm, wet lips teased. Their bodies responded to a desire that had been held at bay for far too long.

"I won't hurt you," Mena promised.

"I won't leave you," Sydney countered as they lay across the bed later that night, talking, kissing, feeling, touching.

The tenderness of their emotional foreplay lingered passionately long after they arrived back home. Mena, unable to wait any more, got on her knees between Sydney's legs, and looked lovingly into the woman's eyes as her fingers gently probed, trying desperately to reach all the way to her lover's soul. Separating the folds of her warm skin, she circled Sydney's swollen and sensitive clitoris with a thumb, causing her to moan. Sydney's pelvis lifted, slid down and all around, arching hungrily in desire, seeking Mena's touch. She was getting close, but Mena wanted something more. She wanted to taste her lover as she came, so Mena lowered her face down between welcoming thighs, and let her lips and tongue take her fingers' place. Soon, they both felt what they'd longed for as Sydney's body tensed, then relaxed, and Mena responded by wrapping her arms around her and pulling her close.

As the high tide of their desire gave way to a peaceful and calm low, Sydney removed a gold chain from around her neck and held it out to Mena, who immediately recognized it as one she'd always worn.

With tears on the verge of spilling over her lids, an emotional Sydney looked longingly at her lover and said, "I want you to have something of mine that has been close to me, to my heart, for so very long. Something that has the scent of me, maybe even part of me." She smiled at her. "Something to remember me when we can't be together, and you are gone."

Stretching to make the ends of the necklace meet, she closed the clasp around Mena's neck, and with the flat fronts of her fingers, splayed the gold across her collarbone.

Moved by both the significance of the gift and the power of the moment, Mena sat back on the bed, looked Sydney in the heart, wrapped her right hand around a few of the links, and whispered, "I'll never take it off." She then pulled her into a hug, and as tears of profound pleasure and joy spilled out from both of their eyes, the women melted into the embrace and fell asleep, savoring the incomparable beauty of a love being born.

CHAPTER 6

In the beginning, the interludes between their reunions blinded them to the realities of what life together for two people accustomed to being alone would look like and become. As with all relationships, the more time the two of them spent together, the more they came to see and know one another—the good, the bad, and the ugly.

Sydney and Mena had gone out to dinner for Chinese at Hunan Gourmet on the Golden Mile in Frederick. Because the campus where Sydney taught was more than an hour away without traffic, she rarely ran into familiar faces around town. Most of her colleagues, who would gladly expound their reasoning, favored proximity and a short commute to a more relaxed and scenic getaway, therefore she hadn't considered the aftermath of a collision between her private and professional lives.

As luck would have it, just as the server put steaming plates of kung pao chicken and moo shu pork on their table, Sydney looked up to see George Miller and a woman she assumed was his wife being ushered directly by their table.

"Fancy meeting you here," George acknowledged her presence with a smile. He stopped at their table and said, "This is my wife, Margaret. Margaret, this is Sydney Foster, a colleague of mine at the university."

"It's a pleasure to meet you."

"Good evening, Mrs. Miller." Sydney stood and moved closer to the woman, so she could give both her customary two-cheeked hug and a more personal receiving.

"Please, dear, call me Margaret," she said as she patted Sydney's hand before turning to go.

Meanwhile, Mena sat forgotten in the shadows until Sydney turned to sit and saw her. "I'm so sorry, Mena, where are my manners?" She called to George and Margaret before they made it to their table and said, "Please forgive me and my rudeness. This is…my friend, Jimena."

"How do you do, dear?" Margaret waved, and George nodded his head in Mena's direction before they moved to sit.

Sydney looked across the table at Mena and apologized profusely. "I'm so sorry, Mena. It's just…I'm not used to you being here, running into people I know, and having to—"

"Expose your 'dirty little secret?'"

Sydney looked at her and shook her head in disbelief at what she perceived to be Mena's continued inability to understand, to comprehend how different their lives were. It was not only years that sometimes separated them, but their distinct life experiences and ways of thinking about themselves and the world. Sydney tried to make conversation, but she gave up after several attempts of addressing a silent void.

Thus, neither one of them spoke another word until the check and fortune cookies arrived. Mena reached for the tab, looked it over, put her American Express in the folder, and placed it at the end of the table.

Not wanting this ill feeling to follow them outside of the restaurant, much less all the way home, Sydney attempted to make amends and bridge the gap by breaking open the folded wafer and playfully sharing her pre-printed destiny with Mena.

She read, "You will take a chance and win…in bed. You do know that's what they say you're supposed to do, right? Add the words 'in bed' to the end of your fortune."

Mena looked at her, unsmiling, unspeaking, obviously still upset.

Sydney wasn't making much progress in lifting the somber mood that had set in.

When the waiter returned with the credit card receipt and thanked them again, Mena asked her, "Are you ready to go?"

Sydney finished chewing the ill-fated fortune's container and said simply, "Yes, I am." Turning to wave goodbye to her friends, she stood and preceded Mena out the door into what would become a volatile night of anger and regret. She couldn't help herself. She was outraged and indignant at what she considered to be an undeserved reaction to a harmless incident.

Safely out of sight and hearing, inside the car, Sydney challenged Mena's behavior. "How dare you? I did nothing wrong. I was merely taken aback by running into a professional colleague, something that almost never happens here, and for only a moment, I forgot my manners."

Mena turned to her. "Oh, is that what it was? A failure of politeness, a polite faux pas, nothing more, nothing less? It couldn't possibly have anything to do with the fact that you're afraid that someone you know might get the idea that I'm more than your friend, could it? Or am I, Syd? How do you think of me? When you're surrounded by others and I'm nowhere near your closet? You seem to live in this veiled otherworld of which I'm not a part, not even as a mention. How can we possibly make it as a couple when you can't even admit that I'm anyone to you, other than a friend? Do you even admit that to yourself? I don't advertise our relationship to the world, and I don't expect you to either, but it would be nice to know you at least stand your ground once you've been seen on it."

With those words hanging in the air, Mena backed out of the parking space. Knowing Sydney had gone from being on the defensive to shutting down for the evening, her typical response to what she perceived as confrontation when it was communication that needed to happen, Mena gave up and dropped it.

Once back at the house, Mena stormed up the stairs and slammed the door to the bedroom. "Why don't you just grow up?" Sydney called up the stairs, knowing it was the one retort Mena hated more than anything. She'd asked her repeatedly, in moments of reflection, not to use it, yet it remained Sydney's number one choice of weapon in her arsenal of verbal offense.

Why was she so stubborn and hard-headed? Why had she continued to insist Mena had been stalled in her development at an early age after being traumatized by the loss of her parents, in a way that she knew hurt her deeply and would send her into an angry outburst? Was there any truth to the accusation that she had internalized hatred of her relationship with a member of the same sex? Of herself? If so, what was she afraid of? Losing her job? The bad things people might say about her? Why should she care what others thought? They didn't live her life, and they certainly wouldn't die her otherwise lonely death.

Sydney sat back in her chair, in need of both a whiskey for her heart and an aspirin for her head.

DESPITE THE THREATS OF THEIR revealing differences, they always kissed and made up. And the end of the school year seemed like the perfect time for them to start their life together. Since Mena was the one who'd first reached out to Sydney, she'd always known she'd be the one to make the move. Besides, Sydney was a tenured professor at her university. Mena would have no problem at all finding a teaching position near what would be her new hometown.

They'd talked about it. Living together and what that might look like for each of them. Of course, the reality of it was more than the shared vacations they'd mostly enjoyed up to that point. While Mena was undeniably excited about the newness of it all, Sydney felt a little unexpectedly encroached upon. Unfortunately, Mena hadn't noticed, and Sydney hadn't shared. That would prove to be their downfall.

"SYD! SYD! WHERE ARE YOU? I've got a sur-prise for you," Mena playfully drew out in song. "Guess what?"

She had come home from work, excited about a plan she'd made for a weekend trip to find empty hangers still swinging from a once-shared cedar rod in their bedroom's walk-in closet. The ringing sound of the wires as their movement caused them to crash into one another left behind an overwhelming sense of mourning, abandonment, and loss. Mena's fears jumped to inevitable conclusions, and her head reeled in desperation as her body quickly followed. Dropping the tickets from her hand, she nearly fell down the stairs on her way to the lower-level guest suite. Sydney was hanging and arranging her clothes with her back to Mena. When what appeared to be the most recent additions of her wardrobe relocation had been situated, she was left with no excuse and turned around.

Mena was stunned into a heartbroken silence. For the longest time, she stood, merely looking at the stranger before her, unable to comprehend the reason for Sydney's inexplicable actions. When she again found words, she pleaded with her, "What happened? Have I done something wrong?"

Sydney lowered her head and moved toward the bed where she sat. Patting a place beside her, she said, "We need to talk, Mena. Please sit down."

Mena refused and remained standing.

"I'm afraid I don't really know where to start."

"How about at the beginning? That's usually a good place."

Sydney smiled, but the gesture failed to reach her eyes. "You know I love you, Mena, I have from the start. Before we ever met in the flesh, our souls had already united. But, and I don't know how to say this without hurting you, I need some space, some alone time."

Mena wasn't sure she understood Sydney's words. She felt a protective shield encircling her body, growing thicker by the minute. Still, she listened. Or, at least, she tried.

"Your constant need for togetherness is suffocating me. I've spent my entire life, until now, mostly by myself. Not that I'm not overjoyed we've found one another, that you've come into my life, it's just...I didn't realize, had no way of knowing, I'd feel like this. So smothered, overwhelmed, and forced into a new way of life."

"Forced? Really, Sydney? Have I forced you, in any way, shape, or form, to do anything you haven't wanted to? Or, at least, that you told me you didn't want?"

"No, of course not. I just need some time. We can still be friends, partners, if you want."

"Friends? If I want? Sydney, what's this all about?" In response to the silence she received, Mena asked, "Is there someone else?"

Sydney looked at her as if she'd just suggested the most ridiculous thing in the world, then shook her head and answered, "No. Of course not."

"Then why are you doing this? Can't we work this out another way? Without you leaving our bedroom, and me?"

"I'm afraid that's impossible. Not right now. And I haven't left you. We're still in the same house."

Without considering the weight of her words, Mena impulsively responded, "That's not the kind of relationship I want." She was reacting with pure, irrational emotion, allowing old fears to rear their ugly heads and open their better-left-shut mouths. She said many things she would later regret to hurt the one who was hurting her, the one she so deeply loved. She let her shattering heart and all her unhealed wounds break open, and a lifetime of uncensored, unbridled anger at being left alone so long ago poured out. In that unguarded moment, she was thirteen again, reliving the pain of her most devastating loss, the unrecognized cause of her perceived clinginess, unwarranted fears, and jealousy—the root of her self- and relationship destruction.

LATER THAT EVENING, AFTER THE rawness of their emotions had been exposed, exhausted, and had worn them down, the two of them sat before the fireplace in numbed silence. Each, in her own way, absorbed the aftermath of what had been revealed when walls that had long ago been built and fortified around their most vulnerable inner selves came crashing down.

A loud *pop* of exploding embers breaking free from a log served as a segue for Mena in what would be her last attempt to draw Sydney into her arms and back from wherever she had gone.

"Look me in the eyes and tell me you don't love me," Mena demanded of her lover, from out of the blues into which she had now looked and had sunk.

Sydney got up from her chair and kneeled on the hard floor. Pulling aside the wire curtain that separated her from the burning flames, she lifted the poker from its place near the hearth and turned the charred stump of ash, giving a last breath of life to the dying fire.

Mena waited.

After Sydney had returned to her chair and settled comfortably against its back, the silence was broken by the cubes that rattled in Sydney's tumbler as she tilted the glass up. Draining the amber liquid, she savored the last drop before facing Mena and forcing words that cut her out.

"Please stop hurting yourself, and me. It's over. It's been proven beyond doubt that we are incompatible. You'll find someone else to love."

At that precise moment, the log shifted, tilted, and slid into the ashes below.

Sydney leaned back in the recliner and pushed the footrest up, refusing to look anywhere but into the flames. Perhaps in search of some source of comfort, she reached for what she'd forgotten was an empty glass. It was apparent even the warmth of the whiskey would fail to console her now.

Mena merely watched. Saying nothing more, she simply turned and walked away into the dark of the split-level's stairway. Evening had settled over them in a shroud of silence.

They avoided each other intentionally, watching carefully for the surprise of opening doors and unexpected arrivals. Mena stayed out late and rose early. She avoided the only common area between them now, the kitchen, by eating all her meals out. Poor Jenny didn't know what to do. Her allegiances were torn. Her back-and-forths and sad whimpering and whining were sometimes the only sound in the home. Three days later, with a winter storm warning in the forecast, Mena packed up the few things she hadn't left in storage and moved out.

CHAPTER 7

"Can I help you?" the fire captain asked when the door to his office had been pushed open after being lightly knocked upon. He'd been typing up an overdue incident report, tedious and tiring paperwork. Welcoming the opportunity to take a much-needed break, he happily looked up.

Mena approached cautiously, unsure whether she'd made a mistake in coming, but the room wasn't large enough to offer the space or time needed for second thoughts. "My name's Mendoza." She extended her hand in greeting. "Jimena Mendoza. I've seen the posts and know you're in need of help with the fires that are breaking out, and I've just moved back from out of town and have plenty of time on my hands. I thought I'd see if there's anything I can do to help."

The tall, gangly man before her unfolded his body from the creaking chair and stood. He smiled and shook her hand. "I'm Joe Peña. Have a seat." He gestured toward the empty chair in front of his desk and sat back down. "We need all the help we can get. If you're from this area and have spent any time here, then you know fires don't limit themselves to the season of summer." His smile turned into a friendly and warm ear-to-ear grin. He settled back in his chair, and after waiting for her to get a little more comfortable in hers, he went on.

"Thanks for coming in. But before I tell you exactly what would be expected of you as a volunteer firefighter here in our house, I'd like to know you better. So please, tell me a little about yourself." Sensing a certain level of discomfort on her part and reticence in responding, Peña continued, "Let me help you out. You can start by telling me why on earth, of all the seasonal jobs you could choose," he paused to tick off a few, "lifeguarding at the Y, summer camp, Dippin' Dots at the ice cream parlor," he smiled, then resumed, "you'd want such a dangerous and demanding unpaid job." He leaned back in his seat and propped his feet up. With his fingers laced together behind his head, he showed no sign of being in a hurry to get back to what he'd been doing, and he waited for her to open up.

"Yuma is my hometown and, although I've been away for a while, I know the devastation fires can bring, the force of nature's fury. I've seen how careless many people are. The random acts of ignorance they practice, despite knowing what can happen here, where it's often so dry and hot." She paused, then went on, "I also know that changes were made some time ago in the way fires are managed, and that the forests, especially in the northern part of the state and across all the west, have become overgrown with grasses and brush, fuels that used to be regularly burned off. The heat alone on the many triple-digit days we experience here is enough to make such tinder spontaneously combust. But even without that, there are plenty of intentionally set fires, automobile tailpipes, and bolts of lightning to get them going with little more than a spark."

Peña smiled, pleased with her awareness of the seriousness of the situation. Although Yuma itself was replete with dry washes and desolate highways, one needn't travel far to find sites where they have wreaked devastation. Laguna and Mittry Lake, even on the Fort Yuma Indian Reservation where former Bureau of Indian Affairs employees who had been contracted on an as-needed basis had set fires on tribal and Bureau of Land Management acreage to be hired for the increased pay of a quick-response. Humans aside, the area was a magnet for thunderclouds and severe storms, and there was no controlling Mother Nature.

He reached for a set of keys that hung from a wooden peg beside the room's sole curtained window, complements of a doting and domestic ladylove. "You've come to the right place, Mendoza, follow me," he invited as he pushed his chair back once again and stood.

He took her out the door and down a long, narrow hall, past a lone combination ladder and pumper truck, pointing out rooms and introducing her to a trio of men who stood next to a collection of red helmets and yellow turnout coats. They stopped at a large, open bay in which tires were laid out, artificial inclines had been created, and dangling ropes had been hung.

"This is where we train and stay fit when we have to stick close to home and wait for calls. Speed, agility, and endurance, among other strengths and abilities, are periodically tested here in timed trial exercises and runs. In our line of duty, none of us can afford being out of shape or facing an obstacle we can't overcome. The people we pledge to protect and serve depend on us."

He looked her over, sizing her up for the job.

"It's important that every man—and woman—" he smiled and continued, "on the line is prepared and able to handle everything from a smoldering ember to a full-out and enraged blowup. Whether confined to an unoccupied, dilapidated shack of a building in the middle of a football field of asphalt or running free in the wild, racing toward an over-populated and dense civilization."

Their eyes met, and she nodded once in understanding and agreement.

He walked on, pointing to a pile of overstuffed sacks lined up against a painted block wall. "See those over there? Each one weighs between twenty-five and forty-five pounds, give or take an ounce, a weight every member of our crew is expected to be able to carry over those hills." He pointed back at the inclines. "And up and down ladders that extend to a height at least two stories tall."

As they rounded the corner and entered the truck room from the rear, Mena saw a series of rolled hoses off to the side. "And, of course, you'd have to learn to roll and be able to wield and carry those." He pointed to them, then flipped a thumb back toward the engine. "And ready gear for each truck. We also make house calls, you know."

IT WASN'T LONG BEFORE MENA had secured a teaching position. It was a profession that always suffered needs and never experienced a surplus. But she continued to fight fires on weekends until the winter months passed and spring gave way to the end of the academic year and the relentless heat of an unbearable desert sun. She'd no sooner packed up her classroom for the year when structure fires were outnumbered by calls of the wild, and it was time for her to pack her bags and go where duty called.

"GRAB YOUR GEAR AND GET moving. We're hiking in."

The last of the trucks had just pulled in on the gravel at the base of the mountain they'd be climbing that day. Doors were slammed shut as the crew piled out and reached for the tools of their trade. Lucky for their lungs, the worst of the smoke was still far away. It was a steep climb, especially taxing for the rookies not yet conditioned to the rigors of their work or the challenges of the terrain, made more difficult when they were laden down with the extra weight of shovels, saws wrapped in heavy chains, and five-gallon water jugs.

After what seemed like an eternal march, the crew leader at the helm stopped and turned to face them. "That's good for now. We'll start here. Ready on line. Follow the yellow shirt to your right. Don't wear yourselves out, but do try to keep a steady pace. Let's go!"

"A PESO FOR YOUR THOUGHTS, Mendoza." A hand placed gently on her shoulder invited Mena to turn around.

"Isa, I didn't hear you come up." She paused for a few seconds, rearranging her thoughts.

"I was just thinking about the fires. So many so soon, with no storms, no dry lightning, or strikes of any kind."

Although Salas knew that wasn't really what had been on the woman's mind, she also knew there was no way to get Mendoza to open up. She would when and if she became ready, which wasn't often, so she let it drop. "I know, right. I mean, it seems like there's been one right after the other. Anyway, I just wanted to say *hey*. I'm being moved further down the line."

Salas smiled at her and waved goodbye, noticing Mena had already returned to her faraway thoughts.

It was only the second week of June, and the earth at her feet had already been sucked dry by a brutal Arizona sun, relentless with its scorching heat and the burning rays it hurled down from cloudless skies. The canopy provided by the branches of the trees kept them mostly shielded, but it also blocked any chance for a cooling breeze that might come down from above. Reaching down for the canteen she had clipped at her side, Mena tipped the aluminum flask up. When her parched throat and cracked lips were satisfied, she emptied the rest of the refreshing liquid over the top of her pounding head in an effort to drown out her surfacing thoughts. Instead, the cascade merely added to the force of the waters within, upon which her memories now freely flowed.

The inescapable pull of the swift current carried her up over the banks of the Gila River through winding canyons and over rocky mountaintops. Back in time to a place where, and to a woman with whom, she'd finally discovered the depth and experienced the true meaning of love.

A COLD, YET COMFORTING SHIVER ran down her spine as she closed her eyes and felt the winds pick up. When she reopened them, she found herself surrounded by the natural beauty of a landscape covered with a blanket of glistening and freshly fallen snow. In her hands, the cool metal gave way to a steaming mug of marshmallow-topped hot cocoa, around which reddened and numbing fingers curled as she stepped back to admire the freezing sculpture onto which she'd just added the finishing touches: a woolen hat she'd bought during a surprise winter sleet storm, a brightly colored scarf, and her cherished Oakleys, now perched comically across the smooth bridge of an icicle nose.

In that one unforgettable moment of pure and simple pleasure that would be frozen into her mind forever, Mena smiled and looked up. Beyond the window's frosty barrier, further still than the hearth's warm and inviting glow, sat a woman. Her face was fixated upon and illuminated by the halo cast from the small rectangular screen at which she stared, oblivious to all but her own innermost thoughts.

"MENDOZA!"

She snapped her head, still dripping wet, in the direction of the unwelcome and intruding voice. With piercing and penetrating eyes, she glared at the man responsible for interrupting a feeling she wasn't ready to abandon or let go.

"I've been calling you for the last twenty minutes." The man jerked his hand in the direction of her radio, which she knew hadn't squawked once. "Now that you've finally decided to grace me with your attention, have you seen Selitto? I can't find him anywhere. He was supposed to relieve Gonzalez over an hour ago."

Seth Henderson, the six-foot-two, blond, blue-eyed, and brawny—albeit, mostly brainless—lumberjack loomed over her, effectively blocking the slant of a sun that had found its way through the foliage overhead. He momentarily blinded her by the light that ricocheted off the shovel he shouldered near a diamond-studded lobe.

"No tools on shoulders." She was happy to remind him of one of the first rules they'd learned as probies.

He merely smirked at her, but in spite of her present mood and personal dislike for the man she often found herself digging line with, Mena attempted a forced smile. The corners of her mouth, however, promptly fell in protest as her squinting eyes came to rest on the words rippled across the too-tight T-shirt that stretched across his chest, which included the words *firefighters* and *hoses*. She really didn't want to know what it read. Shaking her head in disbelief, she stooped to tighten the lace of her boot and turned away in disgust.

"I haven't seen him since we cleared the ridge. Check with Larsen over there." She shrugged him off, sharply signaling the way with the wave of a stiff and slightly charred, well-worn yellow glove.

Although she'd signed on with the forest service specifically for, and welcomed, the rigorous, distracting, and physically demanding aspects of the job, sometimes the displays of testosterone simply got to be too much for her, and Mena wondered how long she could go on. In spite of what she'd read and heard, her experience had been that the average firefighter, with very rare exception, not only failed to acknowledge the equality and worth of the women on his squad, but had no qualms about loudly and repeatedly voicing and displaying his belief that the only place for a woman, in what he claimed as his world, was flat on her back, waiting for him in bed at home or, in his shared ad-nauseam fantasies, at the station house on a bunk.

"Don't let him get to you. He's got it in for all women right now. His girlfriend just dumped him. We're not all assholes, you know."

Mena turned to see Joe Peña standing behind her. She hadn't heard him come up, and she wondered how long he'd been there. Warmed by the sincerity of his words, she returned his smile and stood back up.

Indeed, Peña was different. She had liked him from the start. He'd never singled her out or treated her as any less than the other guys. As soon as she'd shown she was tough enough, which was about the same time she'd grown restless and tired of sitting around the station house waiting for a call, he'd convinced her to head up to Montana for three days of Fire Guard School. There, surrounded by a brigade of mint green Forest Service F250s and amidst a bunch of seasonal workers in search of a Red Card—the basic certification a wildland firefighter needed to be paid for their grueling work—she'd found her niche in the wild.

By way of practice fires and written tests, she had learned how to recognize dangerous weather conditions, monitor wind direction, speed, and humidity, and dig a real fire line in the duff. Although she still helped at Yuma's firehouse when at home, she now spent her summers on-call and rotating out to hot zones like Montana, California, Washington, and Oregon. Tomorrow, she was heading to the famed ponderosa pine forests of northern Arizona, where supposed lightning strikes during a recent and severe electrical storm had caused several fires to break out, but now she found she wasn't convinced of their causes.

"Anyway…" Peña went on, "now that we've got this one pretty much under control, we're all getting together tonight at the Pop a Top before we get orders to move on and scatter about. After all, it's not only fire season, but Miller time." He uncapped a nonexistent bottle of brew in mime and poured out his plea: "It'd be nice to have the whole crew there, but that can't happen without you, Mendoza. So say…seven o'clock?"

"I'll try to make it," she said, gathering her gear and heading down the hill toward their makeshift parking lot.

He knew her well enough to know she wouldn't come. She never did, although he went out of his way to make sure the invitation always went out. He watched her walk away, then glanced over at Henderson, who'd stopped to talk to Salas and now had his back facing him. Guys like Seth would always split up a group.

As far as Peña was concerned, it made no difference what gender a firefighter was, or who they chose to go to bed and wake up with. What *did* matter was that a person had your back when you needed them, that they could be counted on when the going got rough, and Mena had proven to be one of the best he'd ever worked with. He'd trust her with his life, if it ever came to it, though he hoped like hell it never would.

BY THE TIME MENA MADE her way back down the mountain, the sun had already begun its descent as night's sentinel prepared to stretch a blanket of stars above the ocotillo and palo verde trees. Far below, the coyotes, foxes, and rattlesnakes readied themselves for a few hours of foraging and play after yet another day spent languishing in the desert dunes in sands scorched by the heat of the midday sun. Having stored and secured the last of her gear in the rear of her Jeep, Mena paused to gaze up at the gorgeous canvas above her head onto which Mother Nature was subtly splashing and boldly brushing red, orange, and lavender hues with colors that burst forth from the direction of the setting sun.

"Isn't it beautiful?" A hand placed gently on Mena's shoulder brought her back to the earth's ground, and she turned to see who it was. As she refocused her attention, a friendly face came into view. Isabel Salas— the only other woman on the crew, a graduate student at Northern Arizona U, and the young woman who'd greeted her earlier—smiled at her from beneath the blue bill of a Lumberjack's cap.

Mena smiled and looked at her, as if for the first time, studying her intently.

Isa didn't look away. On the contrary, her smile and step forward welcomed the lingering attention.

Suddenly uncomfortable with the closeness and undeniable physical provocation caused by the heat of the woman's nearness and touch, Mena stepped back, causing Isa's hand to fall.

From a safer, more comfortable distance, Mena continued her unabashed observation, during which she saw that they shared similar features, no doubt the legacy of distant, yet linked ancestral families. The same skin tone, straight black hair, and shape of eyes that rested atop high, well-defined cheek bones. Isa's mouth, Mena noticed, was distinct; her lips were fuller and more sensuous.

Unnerved by the intensifying stirring within and the embarrassingly evident visible signs of a body reawakening from a long and lonely slumber, Mena abruptly broke her gaze, shuddered, and looked away. But her distress did not go unnoticed.

A smiling Isa reached out and placed a soft and supple hand along the left side of Mena's face in an intimate gesture Mena was neither expecting nor ready for. Mena instinctively jerked away from the solicitous and enticing touch. "We're going out tonight. I know Joe told you. Why don't you come along?"

Mena's cheek still seared from the heat of the woman's palm, and her heart rate had undeniably increased. She was feeling desire deep down, whether she wanted to admit it or not. The two women simply stared at one another in silence for what seemed like an interminably long time, each caught up in her own feelings, a dance that would soon become impossible to deny or resist if they kept running into one another like this.

Fearing the potential aftermath of a relaxing few drinks in the company of such an engaging *mujer*, Mena hesitated only briefly before turning the temptation down. "Not tonight. Maybe some other time."

Clearly disappointed, yet staunchly undaunted, Isa's frown soon turned upside down as she pulled Mena toward her in one last unexpected, intoxicating, and burning embrace before winking and sprinting off happily.

Mena shook her head in a semi-stunned state of disbelief, whether at what had just happened or more at what she'd felt in spite of herself. With a growing smile on her face, she jumped in her Jeep, turned the key in the ignition, and popped the clutch.

CHAPTER 8

THE CRUNCH OF LOOSE GRAVEL and slight squeal of underinflated tires announced Mena's return home. Chesa, a spaniel stray she'd adopted from a rescue only months before and named for the Chesapeake, a body of Maryland water she'd quickly come to love, stood looking out the bay window of the rented brick rancher, her tail wagging in anticipation and welcome.

As she unloaded her gear, Mena again looked up. No longer the large celestial body she'd admired along the way home, the moon was now smaller, whiter, brighter, and higher up. Although not quite full, it still commanded its place in a beautiful night sky splattered generously with stars.

She dropped everything just inside the door, and with a "Hey, girl," bent to pat the dog's head. In return, Chesa danced, licked, sneezed, and grunted her love. Just then, a black-and-white streak of feline lightning raced into the room. Emi, her other baby, a twelve-week-old tuxedo, darted across the floor, sending Chesa into a jealous frenzy of barks, slides, and snorts. To steal back all the attention, the dog nosed her way into Mena's palm, who took that opportunity to snap on the retractable leash in preparation for her nightly walk.

As Chesa tired herself out chasing lizards down the driveway and across the neatly manicured and thirsty lawn, Mena emptied frogs out of the dog's water bowl and pulled out her cell phone to check for messages, and found no one had called. She wasn't sure what she had expected, or who she thought might call, since she rarely gave her number out, but she was somehow disappointed and felt terribly alone.

She had no one to blame but herself; both Joe and Isa had gone out of their way to get her to join them for a night on the town. *Oh, well*, she decided. They were better off without her along. She didn't think she'd be such good company and didn't want to bring the rest of them down.

Back inside, the fearless feline furball awaited their return at the door, where upon their reentry, he pulled back, then pounced. Mena set Chesa free and scooped the kitten up in one hand, holding him close to her heart. "Y tú, Emiliano Zapata, gato de la revolución, what spoils of war have you left for me today?" Looking around, she surveyed the damage. A pile of books now balanced precariously in the den, toilet paper trailed across the end of the hallway, and dirt tracks from the jade plant served as testimony to the cat's exploration.

"Ay, gatito. ¿Qué voy a hacer contigo? What am I gonna do with you, eh?" The cat purred loudly as she kissed his head, then arched and twisted his way to tumble toward more mischief down on the floor.

Despite her canine and feline companions, Mena had no sooner closed the door behind her when the silence and loneliness engulfed her with its own demand for attention. It had taken her a long time to even want to attempt to make the cold and empty house a home. It was still furnished with only the barest of necessities: a bed, a sofa, a television, a stereo, a few knick-knacks, and some kitchen stuff. The animals helped, but not quite enough.

She pulled her keys out of her pocket, tossed them onto the kitchen counter, glanced at the mail she'd picked up on her way in, and made a detour to turn the television on. As the news anchor informed all tuned in of the latest local and breaking news, she dodged the affection-seeking and playful animals and made her way to the bath down the hall.

Peeling off her grimy shirt, she kicked her boots to the corner, stepped out of her ripped and faded jeans, and slid into the soothing stream of the shower's spray. There, beneath the calming cascade of water, her fatigued body relaxed with her weary soul. That was when the words returned to her memory like a knife thrust deep into her core.

"El amor se va. Love goes away."

Mena's heart raced, and her eyes snapped open wide as she reached for the valve to shut the water off in a near panic. Grabbing the edge of the towel, she pulled it down from atop the ledge of the stall, wrapped it around her chilled body, and leaped out the door of the steamy and suffocating glass enclosure. Leaving small puddles in her wake, she hurried across the hall to her bedroom. Feeling the surge from deep within gaining force, she fought to push the growing wave of emotion down.

Knowing that her only hope was distraction, Mena tossed the towel aside and grabbed clothes from the closet. After pulling on a clean pair of socks and jeans, she snatched up her boots and keys. With the button-down hanging open and her hair uncombed and dripping wet, she ran out the door.

Why? Why were these thoughts of Sydney returning now, when she hadn't thought of her in so long?

EVEN HER FAVORITE MEXICAN ROCKER of all time, Alejandra Guzmán, conspired against her tonight, as the woman's words screamed the echo of her heartache from the Jeep's sound system. Although she had to agree with the song's title—Sydney had, indeed, been her worst mistake—she was unable to bear anymore and turned off the radio.

She'd been exhausted less than a half-hour earlier, but now her adrenaline was pumping. With no conscious destination in mind when she left the house, she wasn't surprised to find herself where she'd ended up. She was, however, surprised to see the place was packed. It made sense, since it was Friday night, and it was the only bar around. Finding no place to park, she pulled out of the overflowing lot and circled the block. Finally, a Mustang peeled away from the curb with a screech that drew attention to a driver and passenger who could be seen moving and grooving in the front seats, matching the rhythm of the car's thumping stereo.

It took Mena's eyes a few minutes to adjust to the dim and smoky haze that clouded the small and stale room. The stench of beer, cigarette smoke, and sweat competed with a myriad of aftershaves, colognes, and perfumes. Once she could see again, she first focused on a small group huddled around the green felt top of a six-pocket table, then her eyes passed onto a pair of lonely and soon-to-be lovers on some nearby stools, until they came to rest upon some friendly and familiar faces in a corner booth: those of Isa, Glenn, Kevin, and Juan.

Still unseen by them, and not much of a party or bar girl herself, Mena hesitated by the door, second-guessing her real reason for coming. The decision as to whether she'd stay was soon made for her by the arrival of an overjoyed and somewhat-intoxicated Isa.

"Mena, I'm so glad to see you." The woman smiled, threw her arms around her in a full-body hug, and said with the slurring of a slight beer-buzz. "What made you change your mind? Don't get me wrong, I'm glad you came, just curious."

Mena released herself from the confines of Isa's arms and said, "After I got home and cleaned up, I realized I wasn't quite ready to call it a night. So I thought, why not?"

"That's the spirit." Isa quickly took her by the hand and led her across the room.

"Here! Here!" Peña, Gonzalez, Selitto, and, *oh God, not him*, Henderson cheered her arrival, ordered another pitcher, and motioned the women over as they themselves, with darts in hand, rejoined the rest of the group.

While Mena and the guys talked shop about the fire and their next assignments, Isa made her way over to the jukebox. She lingered there for a while, taking her time to make her selection of songs. She periodically looked up from the musical menu to glance over and smile at Mena, who not only saw, but feared and resisted her pull.

Saved by the sudden urge of a cowboy's determination, Mena watched as Isa was swept off her feet and onto the dance floor.

Was it her imagination, or had the song been chosen for its message? Isa appeared to be more interested in looking around the man's side and directly at her as the Randy Rogers Band sang, "Kiss Me in the Dark."

An embarrassed Mena felt her ears redden and looked away, but she hadn't averted her gaze fast enough. Isa wasn't the only one who had seen her watching their every move; Peña, too, had witnessed the exchange. He watched as Mena looked down at the table's top, then again lifted her eyes. While taking a long pull on her beer, she turned her attention back toward Isa out on the floor.

Although she smiled at the cowboy from time to time, Mena was relieved to see that Isa kept a respectable distance between their bodies, one reserved for the indifference of an uninterested stranger.

Unable, for the moment, to do any more, Mena gave free rein to her imagination. As the rest of the room faded away, she was the one there on the floor with Isa, whose hands repositioned themselves up around Mena's neck and whose body moved in closer. She smelled the sweet scent of her perfume and could almost taste her.

During her state of distraction, Mena failed to notice the others had gotten up and moved to the pool table, where they were now chalking sticks and racking balls. But Isa had seen, and knowing time was of the essence, she thanked her dance partner, excused herself, and headed back to Mena's side, where she hoped she'd finally have her to herself for a few minutes.

Unsure which glass had been hers and figuring whatever beer might be left in it would likely be lukewarm anyway, she followed Mena's lead. She reached over, grabbed her bottle, and held it up, signaling to the server that she'd like a longneck.

She pulled her hair back and fanned herself with a menu. "It may not have looked like I moved enough out there to work up a sweat, but I have a thirst that is desperate to be quenched." With slightly narrowed eyes and a coy smile, Isa moistened her lips with her tongue. Thankfully, the beer she'd ordered was delivered. Isa ran the lime wedge along the bottle's top before squeezing it in and taking a drink.

"Ah," she exclaimed, "relief." She looked back at Mena. "You know, I think this is the first chance we've ever had to be alone."

Mena turned her head slightly away but maintained eye contact.

"So, am I gonna have to carry on this one-sided conversation all evening? Is it me? Am I bad company?"

Finally, Mena joined in. "It's not you, Isa. It's me. I guess I've forgotten how to be sociable. I don't get out much. I'm a little rusty."

"Well, you can pretty much start anywhere and say anything. I know nothing about you. Other than that, you look damn good when you're out on the line, all hot and sweaty and a little dirty."

That brought forth a hearty laugh from Mena, who said, "Maybe I shouldn't have showered."

"Oh, I never said you weren't equally as fine cleaned up and fresh, did I?"

Mena hoped it was too dark for Isa to see the blush creeping onto her face as their small talk took a flirtatious turn. And, although her mind and body urged her to go with the flow, her heart wasn't quite following in the same way, so she steered their sharing in another direction. "So, you're in college?"

"Grad school, actually. At the University of Northern Arizona. In the summer, I have more of an opportunity to be flexible with my location."

"What are you studying?"

"Forestry. I don't know that I want to be a career wildland firefighter, but I do hope to find where I fit in somewhere in the great outdoors. I love everything there is about it." She lifted her Corona to her lips and looked over the top of the bottle, her eyes never leaving Mena's. "What about you?"

Mena wasn't sure how much she wanted to share with Isa. After all, she was practically a stranger. And a much younger one, at that.

The attraction she felt now was out of the ordinary for her. It could be explosive and dangerous.

"I finished my first round of schooling when I decided I wanted to be a teacher."

Isa, intrigued, asked, "Subject? Grade?"

"Middle school, Spanish. It's a long story."

"Tell me, how does one go from fighting fires in the classroom, which I'm told teaching is sometimes like, to battling real-life blazes? I only have the experience as a student, and I certainly don't think it's something I could or would ever want to do."

Mena laughed. "Believe me, it wasn't anything I'd planned on. It just kinda happened that way."

"Go on. Now I have to know. If it wasn't a childhood ambition and the answer you always gave when asked what you wanted to be when you grow up, how did your life take you that way?"

What the hell? Mena thought. *What could it hurt?* "You see, there was a woman…"

The laughter that shook Isa's whole being surprised Mena. "There always is," she said, "and she's often the beginning and the end. Go on. This should be a good one."

"We met in an unusual…well, a different way."

"Online? In the checkout of a store?"

"She was a writer, and I happened upon one of her books."

"Is this fiction or reality? It's starting to sound like a romantic fantasy."

"It's a true story. For some reason, after reading her novel, I felt oddly compelled to connect with her. The first thing I did was look to see what else she'd written. A quick visit to Amazon showed she had written several other books, and her bio revealed where she was teaching. So I went to that website, searched there, and found her. It was actually pretty easy."

"Stalker." Isa smiled around her bottle as she lifted it for another drink.

"Yes, we later laughed about how it all played out. Anyway, I fired off an email to the address I found there, and within a few minutes, she wrote back. And that's how it all started. How we met."

"Sounds like *Serendipity* to me. Have you ever seen the movie?"

"I haven't."

"Maybe you should check it out sometime. It's worth it for Kate Beckinsale alone, she's such a hottie. Aside from her, it's a cute and awesome rom-com, but it's already sounding like your story could rival its screenplay." Isa looked up as the rest of the crew boisterously headed their way.

Peña asked, "You firefighters ready to roll? We've got an early start tomorrow to make it to Flagstaff before too much of the day has wasted away."

Isa and Mena stood at the same time, but Isa's move was not as smooth; it involved a little sway.

"Are you okay?" Peña asked her.

"Yeah. I just might have had a little too much to drink, but don't worry, I'll be okay by morning."

With a puckered forehead, Peña looked at Mena, pulled his keys out of his pocket, and jangled them, hoping she'd get the message.

She did. "Isa, why don't you let one of us take you home?"

Isa looked at Mena before turning to the rest of her friends. "That's really not necessary. I promise I'm okay."

"We'd just feel better knowing you arrived safely. Please."

"What about my car?"

Peña was quick to jump in. "Gonzalez and I rode together. I can drive you and your car to your place, then he and I will head back to the station so I can pick up my truck. It's not at all out of the way."

making minimal eye contact, lowered her head and handed over her Honda's keys. "If you insist, but I'd rather Mena took me home."

Joe looked at Mena who nodded, happy to oblige Isa's request, all the while questioning the reason it was made.

On the way to Isa's apartment, Mena looked over at her passenger, eyeing her warily, wondering if she'd just been played.

THEY BARELY MADE IT BEHIND closed doors before Isa was all over Mena, kissing, licking, and gently biting her. Mena tried to get her to settle down and into bed; Isa was ready, willing, and seemingly stable enough on her feet to make that happen. But they failed to make it quite that far, finding themselves stalled in the living room instead. With the same soft, full, sensual lips and silky skin Mena had admired earlier in the day, a scent so sweet, and her own desire to put her past behind her and move on with her life, a worked-up Mena's defenses were no match for the intoxicating girl. All it took was a little push and pull, and along with her zipper, she soon allowed herself to be worked down to the floor.

When Mena's jeans were out of the way, Isa tried to get her hands inside.

Mena knew once she did, she'd find she'd had her moist for hours. So Mena grabbed her by the wrist and stopped her hand from reaching its goal. The rest of Isa's body, however, was not nearly as easily dissuaded. With Mena's hands successfully staving off those of Isa, she used her legs instead, wrapping them around any and every part of Mena that she could in an erotic dance of her own.

Isa disentangled herself just long enough to stand and push in a CD before reaching for Mena, to pull her up off the floor. The sexy, seductive, and sensual moves of Isa's body as they kept time with Shakira's "Chantaje" were more than a weakening Mena could resist. A growing desire had her returning the fire, as her pent-up passion exploded.

"Yeah, that's it, baby. That's how I like it. Show me what I know you're made of." Now it was Mena who was intoxicated, not by drink, but by lustful desire. She allowed Isa to lead her to the sofa, where she sat her—gently but firmly—down and stoked the flame with the help of a downward gyration of her body in a lap dance that teased, stopping only inches short of touch. The feeling Mena was experiencing was teetering on the brink between pleasure and torture.

Just when Mena thought she couldn't stand it anymore. Isa leaned over her face and danced faster. Her unbound breasts shook provocatively beneath the cotton blend of her top. Mena, now a willing participant in this seductive game, moved her hands up to cup and caress Isa's tits. Using her thumbs, she circled what proved to be generously responsive and hardening nipples. One by one, Isa tantalized her by slowly undoing the buttons of her blouse and shaking her beautiful, firm, and full breasts close to but not quite within reach of Mena's salivating mouth, leaving her quietly moaning with the ache of desire.

Once in bed, however, it was Mena who pinned Isa down, rolled on top, and took charge. She wasn't sure when it had happened, but in her mind, it was Sydney who lay beneath her, whose clothes she slowly removed, whose legs she gently spread and entered, and around whose hardened nipples her tongue now feverishly swirled.

As daylight dawned, a guilt-stricken Mena, her face wet with tears and her soul drowning in shame and sorrow, stared at Isa on the bed beside her. Feeling like she'd somehow broken a promise to herself and betrayed the one she still very much loved, she silently dressed and quietly slipped out the door.

CHAPTER 9

AT THE SAME TIME MENA was closing that door, Sydney was opening another. The first thing she noticed was that the wooden plaque on the wall beside it was a slightly lighter shade of blue than she recalled. *Perhaps it's been painted since then,* she thought. It had been a while since she'd last been there. Elizabeth M. Sheldon, LCSW it read. She let her fingers feel the coarse texture of the burned inlay letters before turning the knob.

Entering the foyer, she felt oddly comforted, like she was coming home.

As she listened to the peaceful, calming sounds of Enya's "Only Time" mixed with the soothing fall of a fountain's water, a figure appeared at the top of the stairs.

"Sydney?" Liz's voice floated down toward her as she descended with sparkling eyes and a broad smile. "I want to say it's good to see you. Unfortunately, the nature of my profession usually only brings familiar faces my way during times of trouble. Still, it *is* good to see you." Liz extended her hand in greeting, pulled Sydney into the warmth of a friendly hug, and invited, "C'mon up."

Sydney followed behind, recalling the trouble she'd once had finding a counselor with whom she felt comfortable. Sometimes she truly believed in fate, for it just so happened that she'd found Liz's photo in an article on her and the therapies she offered in the newspaper as part of a series that ran during mental health awareness month. Her practice was part of a group of four women who offered the perfect combination of mind-body health services. Some, like Liz, were even lesbians. Thank God! Straight women just couldn't comprehend why it was so important to find someone who could relate personally to the special circumstances of a double dose of estrogen when two women were in love.

The stars had lined up for her the day she happened upon that feature story. Her time and prior work with Liz had done her wonders. Even her distant sister, Jules, had noticed the change in her and told her so. If only Sydney could have succeeded in convincing Jules to give counseling a chance herself. After all, she'd been around the same lecherous uncle in her youth, so who knew? Although Jules loved Sydney in her way, when Sydney had finally summoned the courage to come out to her, she had been hurtfully disappointed when her sibling's response had been, "Just please don't talk about it. I don't want to know." More recently, after Sydney had contacted her for validation of a therapeutic revelation, instead of supporting her, Jules had riled at her for airing the family's dirty laundry with a stranger and told her to "Let it go." How could she make her understand that's what she was trying to do by bringing it up?

Such were the many musings in her mind as the two of them reached their destination on the second floor.

Sydney chose the chair she'd always sat in, awaiting her cue for when and where to start. Liz helped her out. "You told me a little about why you wanted to see me when you called the other day. I must admit, I was somewhat surprised when I picked up your message. Although, I did feel like we hadn't quite finished our work together when we ended last time." Sydney nodded and Liz prompted her, "Can you tell me more?"

She started by telling her about the thoughts and memories plaguing her, about how they were keeping her from concentrating, and her increasing inability to focus on her work and writing. Liz listened intently, nodded her head, stopped her when she needed clarification, and occasionally took notes as Sydney filled in the gap that had since been her life.

When she finished telling her story, Liz responded, "There are many paths we could take with our exploration, but it sounds to me like what you're most interested in is freeing yourself from the memories that are, for whatever reason, returning to and flooding your mind. Am I right? I think you know, however, that for that to happen, we're going to have to look at each of them carefully and try to figure out what's really troubling you. By the way, how are you sleeping?"

Sydney honestly responded, "Mostly, I'm not."

"So I guess there are no insightful dreams to offer grist for the mill with which we can start?"

Ah, now Sydney understood. Given the importance of their previous discovery by way of interpretation, it made sense why Liz would inquire. What she referred to was how, during their first time together, it had taken Sydney six months of counseling and a dream for her to connect her past to her present and overcome the anxiety that had threatened her sanity to the point of her being a basket case of worries and hypochondria. Tied up neatly with stress, nerves, and phobias, together the mental marauders had her with 911 on her speed dial.

Relaxing into the comforting familiarity of the environment, Sydney willingly stepped back in time and closed her eyes, recalling the revelation as she had shared it with Liz, in detail, the morning after it had visited her the first time.

I was walking on the grounds of a country carnival, hand in hand with a little girl, when I realized she was no longer with me. She had vanished, disappeared, gone. Frantically, I began looking for her, circling and circling the enormous field. I ran into others I knew and recognized, asking if they'd seen her. Exhausted by my search, I stopped and looked around. There, in the visible distance, stood a house. Hidden and out of place, it was tucked away in the tree line behind the food tents and Ferris wheel, far from the noisy midway where the carnies and crowds roamed. I rang the bell, and the girl answered the door. She was older, naked, except for a towel wrapped around her hair and another that covered most of her small and fragile body.

"Are you okay?" I immediately asked her. "What are you doing here?"

"They did things to me," is how she responded, all she would say.

Liz's eyes grew big at this revelation, while Sydney seemed completely unaware of the screaming of her mind. She continued to recount in incredible detail, allowing the cloaked memory, never before known to her, to naturally unfold.

When she had finished sharing all she could remember, Liz told her about a theory of dream interpretation that could best be described with the statement, "We are everyone in our dreams." As Sydney attempted to absorb this new perception, Liz asked, "What if you were the little girl in the dream? Did someone, at some time, maybe do something painful, making it hard for you to remember, to you?"

After allowing the question and that way of looking at the meaning of the dream to come more clearly into focus, Sydney told Liz about an incident in her past, a childhood trauma, a true story she'd never shared with anyone. Not because she'd ever forgotten it. She simply hadn't mentioned the molestation because she couldn't see how it had anything to do with what was happening here and now.

"You must have been so afraid."

Sydney, who had never really allowed herself to acknowledge just how alone she had felt, how frightened and ashamed, moved uncomfortably in her chair.

Together, they would later discuss how the abuse had likely been responsible for Sydney's overwhelming need to feel safe, how it was a normal and natural response, and how often abuse manifested itself in a need for control. On that same day, Liz had given her a copy of a workbook entitled The Courage to Heal, for adult survivors of child sexual abuse.

Facing the reality of what she had endured and knowing that so many others had been victims too, that she was not alone in her pain and suffering, had helped her enormously in the understanding of herself. She had seen Liz weekly for a period of about two years before finding herself completely free of the anxiety that had robbed her of precious moments and quality of life before. Not knowing what more to talk about, and feeling like she was spinning her wheels and wasting her money and time, she decided to take a break from counseling.

LEAVING HER MEMORY BEHIND, SYDNEY said, "No, I'm afraid not. If I do dream, I don't remember it."

Liz smiled. "Okay, so tell me exactly why you're here today, why you've come, how I can help."

Sydney settled in the chair and let out a breath she hadn't even known she was holding and began, "I met someone."

Liz cocked her head and pressed her lips together in a quizzical smile. "Tell me about her."

Sydney looked down. "She's gone now. I let her go. Maybe even pushed her out."

This time with a sad smile and brows pulled together, Liz changed one word in her previous sentence and said, "Tell me about it."

And Sydney did. She told her everything. Beginning to end.

WHEN SHE WAS FINISHED, LIZ said, "I'm so sorry, Sydney. Why didn't you come to see me sooner? Before—"

"I didn't know there was a problem. Until it blew up in my face."

"Well, let's see if we can't pick up the pieces. Even if it's too late for you and Mena, if we look closely at each of them, you'll be better prepared for the next time you meet someone."

AS USUAL, SYDNEY LEFT HER weekly session feeling energized, excited, and full of hope.

Just being in Liz's space always forced her to look at herself, see reflection from a different angle and in a new light. With what came up today, she was beginning to see her part in all that had taken place, her role in her relationship's demise. It was a formidable feat Mena had often tried to accomplish, to no avail. Maybe she'd finally had a breakthrough, or at least a discovery that would derail what she feared would be a total breakdown.

Hitting the remote door lock, she made her way to her Mazda's driver's side. Amazingly, the sky had opened up once again, and what had been merely a shower of sprinkles was turning into a downpour of pelting drops. On a pretty day, she loved the drive. Just outside of the limits of the growing town, still relatively small, there were stables of beautiful quarter horses between her land and the city's end, marked by the red roof of the Pizza Hut.

On dreary, gray days like this, she preferred to be at home; not that she had an aversion to getting wet, but because she enjoyed the rain's ability to wash over her defenses while in the solitude of her private haven, where she was better able to simply let it.

She carried her briefcase to the study, where she found Jenny curled up in her bed. "What? I'm too familiar for even a greeting these days?"

The dog's response was a thump of her tail on the floor, but she didn't even raise her head. *Odd,* Sydney thought. *Maybe she's tired.* She shrugged off the out of the ordinary behavior and settled in the chair with the best view of the backyard, a place to where she often retreated both physically and mentally when she needed to write, think, or be alone.

The wind whistled, then howled, as it blew more intensely through the treetops, causing the willow's branches to tangle in their sway, rustling and scattering what remained of fall's detritus on the ground. Drained and devoid of all life and color, the leaves danced mournfully across the grass as the hollow tubes of the chimes sang more loudly their own sorrowful song.

Sydney stood and walked to the patio door. When Jenny followed, she slid it open and stepped out. She turned to find Jenny still inside, hesitating.

"C'mon, girl. You better go now, before it storms."

Jenny sniffed at the air and slowly pawed her way across the carpet. Once she was outside, her fear subsided as she saw and chased a gray squirrel.

Chilled by a sudden and unseasonably cool breeze, Sydney crossed her arms over her breasts and stared vacantly over the fence to a place where her thoughts had come to rest, far beyond the springtime's earlier warmth and thawing caress at a winter's eve not long ago.

MENA SMILED AT HER FROM *across the room as she closed the door and moved toward the fire, shaking the snow from her hair while removing her coat and gloves. Squatting before the flames, she rubbed her hands together and gave them a warming blow.*

So caught up in her writing, Sydney failed to notice Mena had abandoned her place by the fire. She soon became aware as Mena, who had sneaked up behind her, pulled back the neck of her sweater and began to shake down the remaining ice crystals from one of her thawing gloves.

"Mena!" Sydney squealed as she shivered and squirmed away from her lover's icy touch.

"What, honey? You looked so hot sitting over here, all cozy and covered up, I just thought I'd cool you off." Mena bent over Sydney's shoulder and, with a wink and a seductive grin, kissed Sydney passionately on the neck, ears, and throat, eliciting both a throb of desire from deep within her, as well as an audible moan.

A LOUD CLAP OF THUNDER brought Sydney and her thoughts back to the present. She quickly followed Mother Nature's lead and, bringing her hands together three times, startled even herself as she realized that had been Mena's way of calling the dog home. The sheltie was a gift to her from her former lover. She'd come home with the adorable tri-color pup shortly after reading a book of the love letters exchanged between a former first lady and her reporter *friend.* Jenny came bounding across the yard, as if expecting to see her other mother waiting in her usual place in the hammock. Not surprisingly, the canine seemed confused to find Sydney smiling sadly at her from the deck, all alone.

Giving a whine and a whimper, the dog looked perplexed. With a pained expression of her own, Sydney stooped to scoop up Jenny. Turning her face skyward to a band of dark clouds that had rolled in, she gently rubbed her face against the dog's soft muzzle and whispered quietly, "I love you so."

She had no sooner closed the sliding patio door when the wind picked up. Sheets of rain poured down as thunder boomed and lightning danced all around. Jenny, hypersensitive to atmospheric disturbances, trembled nervously and leaped out of Sydney's protective arms to pace the room. To distract the distraught dog—and herself—Sydney led her up the carpeted stairs to the main level of the house, pausing in the living room to turn on some lamps and, by way of artificial light, hopefully drive away the encroaching gloom and her tormenting mental ghosts.

She stopped at the entertainment center, where she opened the unit's door and perused her CD collection. It was Thursday, paella night. Even her dinners were marked by routine, and thus, it was the Spanish tenor Plácido Domingo whose music she sought. However, the disc her fingers landed upon, she realized, was not the one she sought. It must have been one of Mena's, one she'd apparently left behind, forgotten. She couldn't place the sound by sight, so she put the digital recording into the player and waited for the music to jostle her memory.

"Oh, Mena," Sydney exclaimed as she shook her head with a smile on her face. "I wonder if you've changed at all." She'd often teased that she was *only happy when she was sad*, and while she didn't understand every word of the Spanish song, she understood enough to know the music had been left behind as a message for her. Mena often expressed herself in such a way, and Sydney loved that about her.

After putting water on to boil, removing the ingredients she'd need for the Spanish dish from the pantry and refrigerator, preparing a salad to chill, and choosing a wine, she sat in the breakfast nook, where she'd taken all her meals since Mena had left. Looking out through the bay window's glass over the wooden rail of the second-story deck, she sipped the rioja and thought about how the house she'd shared with Mena had come to be a haven for her: filled, if only for a brief while, with such warmth and profound happiness.

She'd loved it from the moment she'd set eyes on it. They both had. A split-level with beautifully cared for hardwood floors, large windows of various types that let in lots of natural light, a gourmet chef's JennAir island dream kitchen, fireplaces both up and down, and

French doors that led to a great room perfect for writing. The place would have charmed anyone. The realtor had told her as she signed the papers, though she was already sold, that the former owner had been an artist, a painter. From where they received their inspiration clearly showed. Since Sydney had been expressly hoping to find a place in which she might one day retire, repose, and write, she took that as a good sign. She'd found it around Thanksgiving, when the trees in the backyard were still stubbornly in possession of a few colorful leaves, thanks to a mid-Atlantic Indian summer that had lingered well into autumn that year.

Sydney finished eating, carried her dishes to the sink, and took her wine glass with her outside. The storm had passed through quickly and once again lowered the temperature it had left behind. Settling down into the thick cushion she'd placed on the Adirondack, she gave contemplative thought to the pathway her life was now on and to how, over time, despite her own resistance, she had evolved. Her life had always been about routine, for as long as she could remember. With a need to be structured, she demanded not only to know where she was going at all times, but precisely what time she'd get there. She became upset when her schedule or timing was thrown off.

But that all changed when Mena came along. Never before had she been so challenged, so unsettled, so shaken up, felt so alive. She hadn't really realized it at the time, but later, she would come to fear that she had let so many years slip by merely existing, enjoying her work, but not really herself. Mena, so different in so many ways, had breathed into her a new passion for living. She was a yin to her yang, the out-of-balance that countered her, her complement, her opposite. Like morning and night, dark and light, she invigorated her with spontaneity and impulsiveness.

Sydney smiled to herself as she remembered the experience and relived her emotion, only to be accosted by a painful thought. Maybe Liz was right. Maybe it wasn't so much a fear of drowning that had frightened her and caused her reluctance to get in the water when they were on vacation, but that she was afraid to trust, afraid to love.

In the end, their relationship had proven to be a double-edged and well-honed sword. It was those very differences that had drawn them to one another in the beginning that would make a life together for them impossible.

She took another sip of wine, tilted the glass, and looked deep into it. Not at the liquid but staring blindly. She wrapped herself around her swirling thoughts. Mena had often told her that she used liquor as an escape. In the heat of an argument once, Mena had even gone so far as to accuse Sydney of being an alcoholic. When all else failed, she refused to make love to Sydney if she'd been drinking, which quickly became more and more frequent. Looking back, Sydney now wondered how much truth was in those hurtful words. Was it the only way she could be intimate? The only way she could let herself be loved?

Although Sydney had never forgotten the unspeakable things her uncle had said and done to her when she was still a young and innocent child, she had failed to recognize the significant and damaging impact the abuse had had on her ability to be in a romantic relationship as an adult. Unable to accept the tender, gentle touches of her lover, their lovemaking would always turn into a mere physical and sexual encounter. She would demand that Mena bite harder, plunge deeper, until she'd been bruised emotionally by the animalistic arousal and by her unsuspecting lover's equally intense and carnal response. Then, Sydney would mentally and physically pull away from Mena's attempt at afterplay, her gentle and tender want and desire to kiss, hold, and touch.

Sydney, after so many years, had finally sought help. But it was too late, wasn't it? Mena was already gone.

CHAPTER 10

CASTILLO SPREAD THE MAP ACROSS the green pickup's still-warm and ticking hood, as Mendoza, Peña, Gonzalez, Salas, and a few others gathered for a briefing and look at what awaited them. They all donned the official uniforms of forest-green Nomex pants and yellow-orange long-sleeve shirts made of the same heat- and flame-resistant material, some carrying shovels, others toting Pulaskis, and a few lugging chain saws. Similarly dressed firefighters and park service forest rangers raced all around in frantic purposefulness, while radios crackled information and commands, truck emergency lights flashed, and equipment to monitor air temperature, humidity, wind speed, and direction was being checked and set up.

"As you've heard, the winds have picked up and this fire is taking off." Castillo moved his finger up and traced a wide arc that stretched to Flagstaff in the north, around Ashurst and Mormon Lakes to the east and south, westward through Oak Creek Canyon State Park, and right in the thick of the Coconino National Forest. "And, as you can see, it's a very large area. Even with all the help that's come in, we haven't been able to keep up with it, much less get ahead of it, so it's gonna take all we've got and then some."

He circled an area in red near Walnut Canyon National Monument. "Mendoza, Peña, and Walker, I want you guys over here. I've already got some men there now, but it's important that we get a line cleared fast. The fire is heading that way, and we can't afford for it to go any further north. I'm hoping we can get to Lake Mary in time to use that as our southern barrier."

As he then hurriedly turned his attention toward and gave destinations and instructions to Salas, Adams, and a few of the other ground crew, the assigned sawyers made their way with their chain saws far out to the front line. The swampers, responsible for throwing what they cut out of the way, followed closely behind. Mendoza and Peña headed back for their gear and prepared to move out.

Castillo interrupted the next newly assembling crew to call to them before letting them get out of earshot. "Remember to carry your shelters! Although we seem to be far away from the hot zone, as we all know, with conditions like this, we could end up in a firestorm before it's all said and done. Keep your eyes and ears open and tuned in and all your senses on hyperalert. Don't forget to monitor wind and temperature, especially on the hilltops." That being relayed and acknowledged as received, he turned his attention back to his new recruits.

STATISTICALLY, WOMEN COMPRISE ONLY ABOUT five percent of most wildland fire crews, and the usual age range of both the men and women is eighteen- to thirty-five-years-old. Mena, at thirty-four, was noticeably over-the-hill and feeling older in more ways than one. Still, she was glad to have been needed and called to Red Rock near Flagstaff to help. Although she'd hoped the trip would give her some much-needed time away from Isa, around whom she now felt extremely uncomfortable, she soon discovered that she, too, had followed, as had Gonzalez, Peña, and Selitto. So far, she hadn't seen anyone else. She supposed they either had other jobs or families that kept them rooted to one spot.

As for Mena, she loved it up north, and she'd considered moving there several times. There was such a difference in that part of the state. It was so green, so beautiful, a forest of real trees instead of a desert of spiny succulents. She took a moment to inhale. The sweet smell of the towering ponderosa pines, which grew to be more than a hundred feet, with grooved yellow and reddish bark, were what they hoped to salvage with their efforts today. Although, history told them the trees themselves would likely survive the fire. They did so by going through a natural pruning process. Sloughing off their lowest branches served to heighten their crowns. Along with the surrendering of the masses of their blue-green needles and cones to burn on the ground, they provided flashy fuels that ignited quickly and burned rapidly, giving the flames the energy needed to burn through fast before reaching the trees' tops. It was the younger pines they would likely lose. The older generation had developed a thick skin in the form of their protective bark.

"You ready for this one?" Peña asked. "It sure looks like it could be a big one."

"I'm ready," she said.

"Are you sure everything's okay? I've been worried about you since the night we all went out and you took Isa home." He put his hands up as if in surrender. "I don't mean to pry, and what happened is none of my business, but I care about you and want to be sure you're alright."

"It's all good, Joe. No worries needed. I promise."

"Okay, then." He went over their checklist while she surveyed the bed of the pickup to make sure nothing, in their haste, was forgotten.

"Rope?"

"Check."

"Reinharts?"

"Here."

"McLeods?"

"Yep, got 'em."

"Flappers?"

"A few."

"Shake 'n' Bakes?"

"Just like you, Peña. Always thinking about food. No matter where or what." Mena joked to ease the anxiety that always accompanied them as they prepared to put themselves amid bigger and more dangerous fires. When battling them, each member of the crew had to be sure to carry paperback-book-sized fiberglass shelters they could only hope, if deployed, would keep them alive while the fists of hell's furious flames pummeled them from all sides. In the backs of most of their minds, however, the three-pound folded rectangles of what looked like aluminum foil were likened to a crashing jet's flotation devices. If ever there were an impact, or you found yourself in the heat of the fire, you'd be lucky to survive. Like prayer, they offered little more than a mental distraction laced with blind faith and hope. They tried not to think about it.

"Do we know where our safety zone or anchor point is?"

Mena pointed to a place on their map, a roadway, an unburnable area to which they were to go if the flames came at them too fast. The last she'd heard, the worst part of the fire was around the Mormon Lake Ranger District near Mormon Canyon, about thirty miles southeast of Flagstaff. It was a very remote and rugged area, if she remembered well. She'd once, in a rare moment of downtime, spent a few days there painting, putting up signs, and clearing fallen brush.

At least there'd be no distasteful fun wear to contend with here. Even her trusty Timberlands had been traded in for the heavy leather logging boots she wore now. This fire was serious, not nearly as docile as the one she'd just helped put out. The threat was very real. Smokejumpers were helo'd in and Hotshots had been called out. This was what she'd trained for, running the obstacle course hand over hand along forty feet of rope, flipping on a trampoline, all those pull-ups, scaling trees with harnesses, "walking up" their trunks, bringing them down with crosscut and chain saws, and hiking with heavy packs. This is what it was all for. Although Peña and Mendoza's crew would be working the perimeter, the *ring of fire*, there were lots of others in the red of the heat. Still, all their jobs were important. They were responsible for clearing away the ground fuel the fire would otherwise consume and feed off.

Although there weren't any homes in the immediate vicinity, and they could and often did allow such natural fires to burn themselves out, there were too many state parks and lots of opportunities for recreation in the area, and they couldn't be sure how many campers and hikers might be unaware of the danger. And, of course, there were always the foolish few who lived, and sometimes died, for the thrill of defying red flags and warnings. Those, she dared admit, you couldn't feel too sorry about.

"Okay. It looks like we have everything we might need." After securing the tailgate, Peña gave the all-clear to the rest and prepared his crew to move out.

"HOLA, MENA."

Mena inwardly cringed at the sound of Isa's voice. She had dreaded the coming of this moment for days, but she was glad it was here, in a way. She looked up from the field kitchen feast of ribs, beans, and potatoes piled high upon her plate. Grabbing a napkin, she wiped barbecue sauce from the corners of her mouth.

"Mind if I join you?" Isa asked.

Mena waved her hand toward the empty place across the table from her. "It's all yours," she gestured, picking up her drink and washing down her food.

Isa pulled the chair out and took a seat.

Mena decided not to waste time, to take the initiative, "Listen, about the other night…"

"Don't worry about it, Mena. I got what I asked for, and I paid the price for it with one hell of a hangover the next day. Let's just enjoy our meal. God knows we've both earned it today, and I don't know about you, but I'm starving."

Mena looked over at her, trying to decide how much of what she'd said was more than false bravado talking, and concluded Isa merely put up a good face and front. Oh, she was a strong woman, there was no doubt about that, but more so on the outside, to protect a more assailable softness.

But Mena, knowing she'd have no peace until she said what she had to say and could put her remorse, at least verbally, to rest, took a bite of a biscuit and went on. "I'd like to talk to you about it. That is, if you might care to hear what I have to say."

Isa looked up from her plate and put her fork down.

"Not here," Mena clarified, "maybe later, when we've finished stuffing our faces and are in a more private place."

Isa resumed eating and said around a mouthful, "Sure, Mena. Anytime."

Relieved of the pressure for the moment, the two women sat in silence for a while, listening to the conversations of those who surrounded them, mostly strangers who talked about their studies and professions. Some were students, like Isa, studying forestry and fire science. Others were volunteer firefighters, used to battling contained, structural blazes in more urban areas. A few were there for the protection of wildlife. They were the ones sitting closest, talking about how, under normal fire-free circumstances and at their current altitude of about seven thousand feet, chances were they might be fighting for their food with a bobcat, desert bighorn, or mountain lion.

After Isa and Mena had emptied their plates and grown weary of the same repetitive discussions, they cleared their places for the next hungry duo, carried their trash to the can, and headed for the tents they'd earlier pitched in the park service parking lot. It was already half past eight, so Mena thought it best not to waste any more time.

"Isa, I'd just like for you to know that…and it's gonna be hard for you to believe this now, but…I'm not like that. I'm not a bad person. I didn't mean to use or hurt you. It's just…" Mena sighed in exasperation, in search of the right words. "I got caught up in the moment, the feeling, in you. You're such a beautiful, sexy, exciting woman, and…well, I'm attracted to you physically…I'm just not ready emotionally, you know."

"Mena, I already told you. Don't sweat it. We're both big girls, all grown up. It's okay for us to…*play* every once in a while."

Mena returned only a half-smile. "I guess I've spent too many years around nuns and a Catholic school environment to live so guilt-free and not take responsibility for my actions, at least after the fact."

Despite what she was saying, Mena knew Isa hadn't been herself either that night. The provocative teases and sexual gyrations, the aggressive assertiveness she'd displayed, it was all for show and wasn't who she really was. If she were like that, Mena would have seen it, seen her like that with others. After all, she was surrounded by ample opportunity, and if for some reason such displays had managed to elude her detection, she'd have at least heard about it. Isa would have a reputation that, like wildfire, would have ignited and blazed a trail of overheated gossip through the firehouse. Mena herself had witnessed numerous come-ons, invitations, expressions, and flirtations thrown Isa's way. She'd either been oblivious to, ignorant of, not impressed by, or not interested in them at all. If she were like that, maybe Mena wouldn't be feeling quite so badly now.

Mena asked, "So do you think I've ruined our chance of being friends?"

"Of course not, silly."

As they passed the lot where they'd parked their cars, Mena excused herself long enough to walk over to her Jeep and pull out her guitar from beneath the remaining clutter on the back seat. Although the six-string acoustic Gibson had seen better days, she'd had it since her father had given it to her when she'd turned eight. It still served the purpose of helping her convey her thoughts and feelings when her own words seemed too shallow and trite.

"You know," she said to Isa with a smile, "it took me forever to get used to the pain of the steel strings." She laughed. "I almost gave up learning to play because I was too much of a wimp for the pain. My dad told me it would be okay, that I'd get used to it, but I didn't believe it. I never really put my heart into it until it was too late for him to see. On the day he died, I picked up this guitar, and I plucked and strummed and pulled those strings until my fingers bled. I did that every day for the longest time. It was my way of being close to my father, I guess, of keeping him with me. One day, I realized that my fingertips were toughening up. Just like I was."

Mena looked at Isa. She had a smile on her face, but she was fighting to keep the tears of a fond yet painful memory from coming. "I'm sorry, Isa. It's hard for me to make myself vulnerable, to let myself be seen all the way to my heart, to open up. I haven't always been like this, but I've learned it's sometimes better that way. Safer not to share too much. I find it much easier to do so with words on paper or in a song, whether they've been written by me or simply discovered."

Mena placed her hands gently over the hollow mouth of the instrument and let her fingers move the strings as her mind drifted in search of the words she wanted. As usual, they came to her by way of one of her favorite writers. She asked, "Have you ever read any of García Lorca's poems?"

Isa shook her head no.

"He was a wonderful and sensitive Spanish writer who was killed during his country's civil war in the late 1930s. Many believe it was because he was a homosexual. He wrote a beautiful elegy in memory of a friend of his, a *toreador* who died after being gored in the ring. One of his best-known works is called "La guitarra," the guitar. It speaks to the power of this magical instrument and the sorrows of the one who places her hands on its strings. He wrote, 'corazón malherido por cinco espadas,' a heart wounded by five swords. I often wondered why five and not six, until I realized the number referred to the guitarist's fingers and not the guitar's strings."

You didn't deserve the other night. I didn't take you home with the intention of doing what I did. I didn't mean to take advantage of you or mislead you into thinking—"

"My God, Mena." Isa reached out and placed her hand over Mena's to silence the strings, "I know that, and you know that."

"Still, I feel terrible. I really don't know what else to say. I think it's just that... I'm still healing from an old wound, and I have some feelings that I haven't resolved. I need to deal with them before I'll be ready to be with anyone else again, in any way."

"Mena, really, stop beating yourself up. I know you're not like that. Why do you think it is that I'm so attracted to you? You're special, you're…" She stopped herself mid-sentence and smiled. "Who knows? Maybe one of these days, you'll wake up to what you've been missing and see what's right before your eyes." Isa squeezed her arm, smiled, then let go.

They sat and talked for a while, until the moon was high in the sky and they were surrounded by weary firefighters crawling into their tents for a little body rest and shut-eye, and they decided it was time for them to do the same.

CHAPTER 11

AROUSED FROM A DEEP SLEEP by the stirring of her human, Jenny looked up as Sydney lowered her left leg before removing her glasses with one hand and stretching to place the book she'd been reading on the side table with the other.

"C'mon, girl, let's go stretch our bones."

Careful not to drop the bundle she'd picked up, Sydney lifted herself out of the leather chair's comfortable and cooling embrace, forcing the dog from her lap. Outside, a steady drizzle of rain fell for the third straight day. The grass was a vivid green and the hedges, she took note, were badly in need of pruning and shaping. A soaked squirrel, its tail beat nearly as thin as a rat's by the rhythmic fall of the pounding drops, scurried across the deck by the patio door, stopping long enough to unearth the buried treasure of a walnut. With his cheeks stretched to their limits by the spoils of his scavenger hunt, he scampered off contentedly.

Sydney pulled a patio chair toward her on the covered deck and sat near the light on the wall. With a trembling hand, she untied the ribbon with which she'd long ago bound the letters she now held, a lifeline to her past. Turning the top envelope around, she opened the flap and pulled out its contents. Mena had been relentless with her correspondence; she'd written every day, sometimes more. Most were from before they lived together. A few were after their breakup.

The first was a card that read:

You are the person I fall in love with more each day. You are everything I imagined, everything I dreamed of, and all that I need. You are my first thought when I wake up in the morning and my last before sleep comes each night. You are my fantasy and my reality, and forever the love of my life.

Below it, Mena had written:

Why, Syd? What happened? I don't understand. I wish you'd just… please, talk to me.

Sydney hadn't noticed before that the sturdy stock was crinkled, and some of the writing had been smudged. She looked down at the words that had reached out to her. She would forever be haunted by the pain she'd caused.

Can you imagine how I felt? How it hurt me when I found you that day? And to hear what you had to say? I had given up so much. I believed in you. I believed in us.

Mena had written and written, pouring the contents of her suffering soul onto her pages, hoping to make the Sydney she knew and loved come back to her, to no avail. Eventually, the unanswered letters and calls stopped.

Sydney carefully refolded the pages and slid them back into the envelopes from which they'd come, feeling her own eyes begin to tear up.

"HERE'S WHAT I'D LIKE FOR you to do," Liz said in her ongoing effort to get Sydney to consider views other than her own, to make her see and understand the give and take of relationships and the shades of grays that existed between the extremes of black and white. "Put yourself in Mena's shoes. Try to imagine you're a twelve-year-old whose father has just died in surgery. It's the first loss you've known. Then, ten months later, you're slammed again by a second death. Your mother, your comforter and protector, also succumbs to a debilitating illness. How do you feel? In an instant, your world has been unexpectedly turned upside down. To make matters worse, not only do you now have to uproot yourself physically, but in your preadolescent eyes, you're a burden being forced upon a relative who you're convinced doesn't really want you in her home or life."

Liz paused, giving Sydney the chance to let what she'd said sink in, before going on.

"Now, fast forward some eighteen years. You're an adult, involved in a romantic relationship. Let's work first with the Tulum incident. Correct me if I'm wrong, but wasn't that trip with an old friend of yours planned for a time when you and Mena were supposed to be spending more than a week together for the first time?"

Sydney was exasperated when she responded mid-sigh. "Yes, but keep in mind, my trip with Madeline was not merely a visit. We share a history and passion for going on digs and archaeological quests to exotic, faraway places. I'd always wanted to go to that Mayan City in Mexico's southernmost Yucatán peninsula and was overjoyed at the prospect. Madeline had been the one to make all the arrangements. Her call simply came sooner than expected, and Mena found out about the pending trip by overhearing the conversation. Her interrogation of me began as soon as I'd hung up the phone."

Liz smiled woefully before responding. "Keeping her life experience in mind, is it so far of a stretch for you to see how just maybe, in her mind, her feelings were justified? I'm not saying that she didn't overreact, I'm merely trying to get you to see that there is often more than one way to look at every incident." Liz stood and walked over to the bookcase behind her desk. "I have a book I'd like for you to take a look at." She pulled one down from the shelf and handed it to her.

"Not another one. I don't have time for it."

Liz raised her eyebrows, her way of reminding Sydney she was seeing her voluntarily and had asked for help in understanding what had happened to end the love she'd had with Mena, for insight into the demise of their relationship.

Sydney looked at the book in her hands, *When Opposites Attract: Right Brain/Left Brain Relationships and How to Make Them Work* by Rebecca Cutter. She opened the cover and glanced at the inside flap.

"If you take the time to read it," Liz looked at her "you may be surprised to find how well the author is at describing everyday occurrences and differences that plague many couples who suffer from challenges of communication and understanding. I know when I read the first few pages, I couldn't believe how well she'd managed to describe my partner and me, our differences. It was like she'd been there with us and witnessed one of our many messes." Liz smiled. "The question becomes, how much are you willing to compromise? And will your efforts be worth it in the end? But it has to be a two-way street, otherwise you'll reach a dead end."

As they walked together to the door toward the end of their session, Liz asked, "How does the teacher feel about homework? Doing it, not giving and grading it. There are some exercises throughout the pages," she inclined her head toward the book, "that I think might prove useful for our purposes. I'd like for you to take a look and try doing a few. It'll be a great place for us to start next week." She patted her on the back. "Until then."

AFTER A NICE DINNER AND a warm, relaxing bath, Sydney picked up the book and called it an early night by taking it with her to bed. Only a few pages in, indeed, she was amazed at how well Cutter had pictured her and Mena, from Mena's way of literally scattering her thoughts about the room, her archaic need for a paper and pen as opposed to a computer to express them, and Sydney's own reaction of being bothered by a way that was not hers, a way she could never accept or comprehend.

She got so caught up in the similarities that, before she knew it, she'd read more than half the book. Although she could have read more, she knew if she did, she'd suffer the consequences in the morning when the alarm went off.

Reluctantly, she closed the book and placed it on the table by her bed.

MENA PREFERRED TO FILL OUT her incident reports by day's end, while events were still fresh and clear in her mind, even though she carried a pocket-size spiral in her backpack where she jotted down notes and recorded times. As she filled in the blanks with detailed information, something about the most recent fires kept nagging at her mind. She checked the National Oceanic and Atmospheric Administration website for data on lightning strikes. As she suspected, there had been relatively few recorded recently, none that would account for the fires they were currently fighting. She then Googled "Wildfire Origins and Causes" and pored over statistics and investigative techniques she found interesting, tucking them away in her mind.

While it was no secret the majority of wildfires were man-made, whether by accident or intentional, she knew she didn't have anything to take to Peña aside from suspicion and a gut feeling, an internal gnawing.

She put her paperwork away and closed her laptop before unrolling her sleeping bag, on which she merely stretched out. She tried to get some sleep, but she was wound tight by all her thoughts.

SYDNEY SIGHED AND CLOSED THE cover of her laptop. For whatever reason, the words she sought were taunting and teasing her, remaining just out of reach. She'd had a great idea just before she sat down, but as soon as she opened her computer to begin crafting her manuscript's next chapter, the threads that had woven together so beautifully in her mind had tangled, unwoven, then each gone their separate ways, the sentences and thoughts falling irretrievably apart.

"It's no use, girl. It's simply not happening today." Jenny looked up at her as if she understood and could feel her human's pain. If Sydney were to admit it, she hadn't been able to produce anything worth submitting for publication since *The Keeper of Dreams*, an adaptation of one of her earlier novels Mena had helped her rework after it had been requested for a young adult's literature anthology. She didn't even know if it had made the editor's cut, but since it had been solicited, she assumed it was circulating out there in classrooms somewhere.

"El dueño del sueño." She mused at the memory of the piece's title. It centered around an old Yuman's storytelling to keep the history of certain customs of his indigenous peoples alive in their memories. She could see why the editor had wanted it. High school and cultural studies students all over the southwest were being introduced to the original as part of the burgeoning US Latinx literature canon.

She smiled at the memory of how easily their writing had come together, as if it were meant to be. Maybe she just needed to abandon her current pages and start anew. Alas, she lacked inspiration. She had never experienced writer's block. She'd always had characters in her imagination, demanding their stories be put on paper. But those voices had grown silent. What had happened to her? Why was she having so much trouble focusing, concentrating, and writing these days?

Mena had become her muse, her inspiration. Without her, both she and her writing were lost. Their collaboration on her last novel had won it both humanitarian and literary awards. Why hadn't she listened to Madeline when she suggested they attempt to at least salvage a writing partnership? Oh, she knew why. At the time, she wasn't willing to admit she needed Mena, even in that way. As a matter of fact, she'd gone so far as to remove her cowriter's name from the dedication page after their breakup. Where before it had read: "For Jimena Mendoza, who believes in the meaning of dreams," now, on a much more impersonal page, readers saw her revised claim that it had been written "For all oppressed peoples everywhere." It sounded good, to those who didn't know.

Thinking back to her initial dedication, Sydney remembered how animated and excited Mena would get when she'd had what she referred to as a *speaking dream*. She thought of one recurring pattern in particular. Had she not been told of the dreams before they came true, she wasn't sure she would have believed it or put any stock in the visions. But three times, Mena had dreamed of a gambling win, of all things, and three times she had hit a jackpot containing those very numbers. Not to the dollar amount, but within the thousand-dollar range that appeared on her dream slot machine. After that, of course, Mena had prayed for such dreams. However, no amount of presleep thoughts or subliminal recordings could make them appear at will. Sydney had to chuckle to herself. Despite the belief she, herself, had in dreams, foretelling fortunes of that kind was never anything that had crossed her mind.

Maybe what she needed was a getaway. From her thoughts and memories, from the ghosts of the past that remained to haunt her in this place. But where would she go?

CHAPTER 12

Sydney took a few moments to compose both herself and her thoughts before sharing her untold stories, the secrets she'd guarded, with Mena.

"Allyson was my first love. I know I told you about her. Well, I've at least mentioned her name."

Mena nodded.

"But I didn't tell you the whole story of what happened between us." Sydney took a deep breath and steeled her resolve. "We met when we were teenagers. I'd been asked by the nuns at our Catholic boarding school to spend time with her, to be a friend. Although she was a few years younger than I was, she was older than the rest of the girls. And, for whatever reason, she hadn't seemed to fit in. She couldn't find her place, and she wanted to go home. Of course, the sisters didn't want to lose her tuition dollars. In time, I found myself drawn to her. She was enveloped by an aura of sadness that I seemed to connect with. After all, I possessed my own. We spent time together, and it soon became apparent to me that I wanted more than a friendship with her."

Sydney looked at Mena to gauge her level of interest before continuing. "It was so long ago. I no longer remember all the details, but I do know that during one of the hours of angsty tenderness we shared, my heart went out to her. Finding no words that could offer the comfort needed, I consoled her with a kiss. A kiss that she returned." Sydney looked down at her lap and smiled at the apparent warmth of the memory.

"After that, I was simply over the moon. I went home and couldn't sleep that night. All I could think about was that feeling, the feeling of her lips on mine. The feeling of, for the first time, falling in love. It was fairly innocent, after all, we were but young girls." Sydney paused for a moment. "But I was so happy, so overwhelmed, so emotional, so in love. I couldn't believe or understand why she seemed to avoid me the next day until after the last of the other girls had gone off to their dormitories. It was only then that she appeared. And with a friend, not alone. Of course, I knew something was up. She looked so sad and serious. She'd obviously had her own sleepless night and restless day, although, I suspected, for different reasons than my own." Sydney laughed in a way that belied how hurt she'd been then, and how much she still was today.

"She…they…moved to take a seat at one of the dining room tables and, I followed along, rightfully assuming she had something she wanted to say. Given the mood, I feared the worst. Believe me, it was coming. Without a word, Allyson extended a trembling hand my way in which she held a folded piece of paper. I shook as I opened it and read a condemnation of eleven letters, the first of each of the words she could not bring herself to speak aloud or even spell out in their entirety. Somehow, I immediately knew and was able to decipher the barely cryptic code. Since that day, it's been seared into the depths of my heart and soul."

Sydney reached for a scrap of paper and pulled a pen from her purse. On the paper, she wrote, *P.D.K.M.T.W.A.I.I.N.P*, and handed it to Mena. "Would you have known what she was trying to say?" Sydney struggled to control her emotions before answering her own question. "*Please don't kiss me that way anymore, it is not possible.* What was I to think? How was I to feel? As you might imagine, my heart was not only broken, it was completely pulverized. My entire being was crushed. All the happiness I'd allowed myself to feel the day before was no more. It had been replaced by a depth of sadness I didn't realize was possible." Sydney sighed heavily.

"It took all of the strength I had in me to get up from that table and walk away." She appeared to be transported in time, reliving those emotions, that moment, that loss.

"While Ally would revisit me in my thoughts and memories for years after that, I never saw her again. I came up with some excuse for why I couldn't go back to that school, and I transferred to another. I threw myself into my studies, and although I wrote her a library of letters, I buried them deep in my hope chest, where they remained unsent until I burned them all. My schoolgirl studies eventually gave way to college and post-graduate research. It gave me all the excuse I needed to bury myself in libraries and books. These days, computers make it even easier to isolate oneself from others." She looked at Mena with a rather rueful smile.

"Why didn't you ever tell me any of this?" Mena asked.

Sydney looked at her. Her lower lip trembled slightly before she spoke. "I don't know. I wanted to. I just couldn't."

"Had I known, it might have helped me to better understand you, what was happening between us." Jimena shrugged.

"There's more, Mena. Something much bigger I should have shared."

"About your uncle? You told me about that, about him. I already know."

Sydney shook her head. "It wasn't just my studies that I turned to after Allyson. Maybe my change of direction was influenced by my many years at a Catholic school, but I immersed myself in religion and had committed myself to be a Bride of Christ. I thought maybe I was being punished for what I was. That I was wrong to feel that way, to want that kind of love." Sydney looked at Mena, imploring her to understand. "I didn't tell you because I was afraid of what you might think of me. I wasn't sure you'd want to be with me, knowing I'd spent years in a convent, living a contemplative life, praying, searching for answers, and trying to force myself to be a way I was not. In the end, I had no choice but to be true to myself. After six years, I left the order before taking my final vows."

Mena's eyes grew wide, and her brows raised; even her mouth gaped open in shock.

"I wanted to tell you that the day you found me in the closet. I had every intention of telling you, to explain what I was feeling, why I was so overwhelmed. It wasn't really you, Mena. It was me. And I'm not sure I entirely realized it until I entered counseling."

Before Mena had a chance to respond, a nurse walked in and reminded them, "I'm sorry, ladies, but your time together this evening is up. Our patient needs her rest. Visiting hours are over."

Sydney tentatively reached out a hand and let it land on the blanket over Mena's leg, and she gently gave a squeeze before reaching into her purse to pull out a CD. "Con Los Años Que Me Quedan" by Gloria Estefan. "This time, *I'm* leaving *you* with a song. My story, our story, is…to be continued," Sydney promised before she turned toward the door and slowly walked out.

MENA HADN'T SLEPT AT ALL that night. Her mind had been a firestorm of thoughts. *What else had Sydney been going to say? Had there been others? Other loves after Allyson? And what about her time as a novice? So much of it all makes sense now.* But before Mena could reflect any further, Isa came charging in with a cheerful grin, swinging the bag she'd been given days earlier that held Mena's belongings.

"Buenos días, chula. I came by to see how you're doing and to give you back your things."

"Actually, she shouldn't have any jewelry or money here," said Alex, who'd walked in hot on Isa's heels. "There are lots of people in and out, all the time, and we have no place for safekeeping. That's why we give it to someone to take home," she informed them both.

"My bad." Isa hung onto the bag. "But I thought she was being sprung today?" She looked to both of the women with a confused expression on her face.

"Not for another day or so, I'm afraid. I'm sorry. Doctor's orders. He wants to repeat the MRI once more and consult with the neurologist before he signs her walking papers. And, unfortunately, as we've only recently learned, neither one of those can happen today."

Mena shattered Isa's mental reverie by asking her, "Do you think you could hang onto my things until then?"

"No problem," she said.

Since it was clearly visible through the bag she held in front of her, and because it had piqued her curiosity ever since Mena had been brought in, Isa took the opportunity to comment on the necklace. "That's a very pretty gold chain. The link is unusual. I don't believe I've ever seen one like it."

Both Mena and Alex looked at the bag. The tears that shimmered in Mena's eyes told both women all she didn't say. It was a piece of jewelry that came with a story, and, given the reverberating silence that followed Isa's inquiry, it was a very emotional one.

Mena motioned for Isa to hand her the bag. She pulled the chain out and ran it through her fingers. "It was Sydney's. I would have given it back to her when she was here if I'd known she wasn't coming back. But then, I didn't have it, you did." She smiled at Isa.

Beginning to feel like a third wheel, Alex made an excuse for why she should be somewhere else, "Well, ladies, it looks like it's time for me to fly. I only stopped by to check on my star patient." She patted Mena on the arm. "Duty calls me a few wings and floors away, where they're probably wondering where I am, and I'm never late. If you have any other questions, or find you need anything, I'm sure the next nurse on duty here will be able to help either of you." She excused herself by saying, "Enjoy your visit," and left the two alone.

Mena saw her opportunity to change the subject and seized it. "How's it going with the fire? Has it been contained?"

Isa looked at Mena and shook her head. "It's a mess, Mena. Every time we think it's under control, the wind picks up, and there we go again. They've called in all kinds of help. Even smokejumpers are parachuting in."

Mena thought for a minute about what her friend was saying. She decided to share with her what she'd dreamed. "I had a dream about the fire." Isa's eyes widened, so Mena told her about the vision that had come to her during her sleep. "I dreamed that it blew up while you and Peña and a few other guys were trying to make a getaway. The flames closed in too fast, you were trapped, and there was no escape. You had to shake open your shelters. By that time, the heat was incredible, and your skin was blistering."

Mena, who had drifted away with her storytelling, looked at Isa before continuing.

"I was there, in the dream. Well, not *there*, but I was able to see everything. I watched you run until you couldn't anymore. I saw you crying as you fell to your knees. In your hands, you clutched a wooden rosary." Mena's voice revealed the level of her emotional involvement with her dream. "You were right there, but I couldn't reach you. I couldn't do a thing. I felt so helpless. That's when Peña came back for you. He picked you up and carried you to safety."

"Wow. I'd say that was more of a nightmare than a dream. Thank God that's all it was. I can't even imagine coming that close to such a life-and-death experience." Isa shuddered visibly.

"I woke up terrified. Not to scare you or anything, but I'm still afraid it could have been a prescient dream. Please promise me you'll be careful out there."

"I will. There's no other way, believe me."

As she remembered the details and relived her feelings, Mena tuned the rest of what Isa had to say out. She became aware that she'd not been listening to what Isa had been saying when she realized the room had grown quiet and Isa was no longer talking.

"What?" Mena asked when she saw her staring expectantly.

"I *said*, whatever happened between you and Sydney, anyway? I mean, has she gone home? Or is she still here in Arizona? Have you seen her yet this morning?"

"No, I haven't, and I don't know what to make of it. I thought she'd be here first thing." *Especially given last night's revelation.* She wondered why Sydney hadn't returned. She thought she'd be anxious to resume their reunion and continue their conversation, but so far, nada.

Mena remained quiet for a while, then shook her head and shared, "It was all so very strange, having her here. I don't understand it or know how to explain it, but, in a way, I was somehow expecting it."

Isa's eyebrow raised.

Mena tried to explain. "For whatever reason, I'd been experiencing a resurgence of memories. About her, us, our time together. I felt sad, almost like I was in mourning. Then, well, my accident led to my seeing her again. Now I have no idea what to expect, what's going to happen, what's going on."

"I wish I could tell you that I understand, but I have yet to experience such a rite of passage. My relationships thus far have amounted to little more than flings and interludes of intimacy too brief to even be called such."

"Thankfully, for your sake, I don't think all relationships are this complicated. Just make sure you keep open communication. That seems to be the key."

Having said that, Mena realized having the key wasn't always all that was needed to open a door. Especially one that had been impenetrably closed. *Why did Sydney open up like she had, only to disappear again? What is going on with her? Has she reentered my life? Is she hoping for another chance? Does what she shared change anything?*

CHAPTER 13

SYDNEY COULDN'T BELIEVE HER LUCK when her rental car wouldn't start. As it was, she didn't have time to spare. She was due back in Maryland at the university for the first day of classes and couldn't let the chair of her department down. She had always been so dependable. To make matters worse, how would her absence look to Mena now? Just when it appeared their relationship might be on the mend. *Why now?*

Isa had called her to tell her about Mena's accident on the university's phone, and in her worried haste, she'd neglected to write her number down. *Why didn't I add her as a contact in my phone?* She cursed herself. Oh, well. No sense beating herself up about that now. Plan B. She looked up the hospital's website. But last she knew, Mena had still been in the critical care unit. *Had they moved her? I'll just call and see if I can at least get word to her.*

"Flagstaff Medical Center. How may I direct your call?"

After explaining the situation, the receptionist said the best she could do was take the message and pass it along. "I'll do what I can to make sure she gets it."

"Please do. She may even be checking out this morning. I don't know."

Sydney had worried her hair into a mess by running her fingers through it repeatedly as she paced the floor. Patience was never a virtue bestowed upon her, and she was very aware of that now. Still, she thanked the woman and disconnected the call.

What else can I do?

Her thoughts were interrupted by a call from the rental agency in which the representative said they'd have someone over to look at the car right away. And, if need be, they could have a replacement vehicle for her within the hour.

THE DAY FOR MENA'S RELEASE from the hospital had arrived. Dr. Johnson was there to give her a clean bill of health. Alex, who in such a short time had become a friend to both her and Isa, had shown up to send her off. Peña and Salas rolled up to whisk her away in their version of a park service limousine, a recently cleaned pickup truck. There was much cause for celebration: she was going home, and the fire was mostly contained, all but out. But there was still no word or visit from Sydney.

Mena couldn't imagine what could have happened to keep her away. Maybe she was in hiding again after having revealed what she did. *I wonder if there was even more to tell.* Before she left, Mena gave Alex a plant to care for in her absence, a succulent. She laughed, and Mena said, "It won't require as much care as I did."

As she passed by the rest of the staff, she said, "Thank you all, for everything, for taking such good care of me, for your kindness." In turn, they wished her well and raised their hands to wave goodbye as Isa wheeled her out the automatic door, mumbling, "Yet another hospital regulation. Sheesh. Did they ever think if you're not well enough to walk, maybe you shouldn't be leaving?"

"Shut your mouth!" Mena playfully threatened. She was more than ready to go home and get on with her life.

After catching up with Peña and assuring him, at least a dozen times, "I'm fine," Mena felt like she really was, for the first time in a long time. At least, she was starting to be. Maybe all she'd needed was to see Sydney again to get the closure she'd needed, but she wasn't sure more had been opened than closed during their last talk.

THE DRIVE FROM FLAGSTAFF TO Yuma took forever, and while she was happy to see Peña and was grateful for the ride, Mena doubted she was being the best company or seeming very gracious. She hoped they would blame it on all she'd been through or chalk it up to the fact that she was probably tired.

Meanwhile, the hypnotic humming of the truck's tires on the asphalt could be heard loudly during the lulls in conversation between the passenger and driver up front, but Mena was disappointed to find the miles did nothing to distance her from all that had happened in the place she was leaving behind. The fire. The accident. The hospital. Most of all, Sydney, who hadn't returned as she'd promised. *Why? And why hadn't she even called?*

Suddenly, Mena remembered the CD she'd been given. She knew some of Gloria Estefan's stuff, but not that particular song. She'd play it as soon as she got home. She smiled to herself. *So this is how it feels to be on the receiving end.* No matter what the message in the music might be, she knew it wouldn't explain why she hadn't seen or heard from Sydney. Unable to join the efforts on the fire line, she'd need something major to occupy her mind.

After an enthusiastic reunion with Chesa and Emi, and, of course, the requisite goodbyes to her human entourage, Mena couldn't wait to hear what Sydney had to say via Estefan's song. She played it through several times. So far, the only thing time told her was that Sydney had disappeared from her life once again, and without words other than these. The words didn't explain her actions, only confused them more. On one hand, Sydney was asking for a second chance, promising a lifetime of love. But the other hand had apparently waved goodbye. She didn't know what to make of it all. For the time being, she turned the music and memories off and headed to the study.

There was no time like the present to begin distracting herself. The first thing she did was pull up a satellite image of the burn area of the fire closer to home, the one she'd been called out on before she'd headed north to the Coconino.

It was much easier to see from above where the point of origin, the fire's starting place or vortex, likely was. Since all infernos followed a U or V pattern, once that had been determined, the path the flames had followed as they fanned out across the land took shape on the monitor's screen. Next, she looked at maps to see which roadways were closest. When the NOAA stats confirmed what she already knew to be true, that there had been no lightning strikes in the days preceding it, she decided to do a little more digging and conduct some surveillance of her own.

I may not be ready to get out there on the frontlines just yet, but there's no reason I can't sniff around in an area where I've already been. She shoved a couple of water bottles and the computer printouts into her backpack and took off.

THE FIRST THING SHE REALIZED, as she walked the woods, was how much easier it had been to see where a fire had likely started from the outside looking in, or from the upside looking down. From ground zero, where everything looked the same—black, burnt, and barren—it was harder to tell. She decided to start where she was and work her way westward over the burnout until she came to ground that appeared to have been untouched.

The area burned in that direction was much larger than she'd thought. But, as she walked, she saw recognizable evidence that she was headed in the right direction. Remaining vegetation had been bent forward as the fire had roared over, and she saw parts of burned tree debris with one-sided ash buildup.

Finally, she came upon some surviving live green on the verge of the dead black, and she marked the zone where she would begin looking around. She was on the hunt for a needle in a haystack, she knew it, but what else did she have to do right now?

Her work would have been much easier with some help, but she didn't want to burden Isa and wasn't sure who she could trust. So she went it alone, marking off grids and searching for anything that seemed out of place or looked like it could be of significance. A footprint, tire mark, or the remnants of a time-delay device, anything that might have survived the destruction in this otherwise natural environment.

Using a stick, she poked around in the high grasses while snippets of conversations she'd picked up earlier from the guys moved around in her mind and added fuel to the fire of her suspicions. She couldn't seem to quell the uneasy sense that something was very wrong, that this fire had not been a naturally occurring one. There had been too many recently, all within too close a proximity to each other. The crew wasn't getting much of a break. In past years, they'd had lots more downtime. Some of the guys admitted to being grateful for the financial windfall the firestorms brought. "More money in my pocket," they'd said. And it was true. When there were no fires to fight, money earned was tight. That wasn't the case right now. These days, there seemed to be much more boom than bust. There was actually money to burn. And, she wondered, *could that be what this was about?*

As much as she hated to do it, she thought of each of the guys, of the motives they might have for starting the very fires they were putting lives at risk to put out. There were new babies, expensive hobbies, and plenty of wives that liked to shop. But who among them would do such a thing? She would put speculation aside and let the facts and findings figure it out.

WHEN SHE GOT HOME, SHE put her sleuthing aside and tore into the bag she'd picked up from KFC. She hadn't realized how hungry she was. As she devoured a breast and a leg, she noticed the words on the container's side. *There are few problems a bucket of fried chicken can't solve. Okay, Colonel Harland Sanders,* she thought, *I hope you're right. I'm gonna hold you to that promise.* These days, promises didn't mean much.

With that acknowledgment and a full stomach, she fired up another hunt, this one for a paper she'd written after her and Sydney's breakup. It had been written impulsively in response to a call for submissions she'd stumbled upon that was in search of stories about relationships that had started online. Though she'd never sent it in, the words had flowed forth so freely and therapeutically, unlike any she'd ever written before. She'd given it the title, "Love at First Write" and had never shared it with anyone.

Amazingly, she was able to put her hands on it in no time.

"LA VIDA ES SUEÑO." LIFE is a dream, or once upon a time, so wrote a seventeenth-century Spanish playwright. As one with an innate love for literature and an insatiable interest in the workings of the human mind, I delved deeply into the self-assessing of such a thought-provoking drama with "gusto" and "placer," never dreaming I would one day soon experience firsthand the protagonist Segismundo's philosophical musings and a similar surreal state of being as the result of the much more modern words of a contemporary novelist and her creative writing.

This is my story.

ON A SATURDAY AFTERNOON IN late June, Fate and Destiny joined forces with a no-less-than-demonically-divine intervention in my life. A ravenous reader in possession of a voracious appetite, I'd wandered downtown to the public library in search of a little food for thought.

I'd just checked out two armloads of books (some fiction, some not), with characteristic multi-dimensional, multi-faceted personalities in settings that ranged from the great outdoor Arizona desert to the great indoor therapeutic couch.

And it was closing time.

Laden low by my very eclectic tri-weekly selection, the weight of many words, I struggled to hold my head up high and squinted against the bright glass door glare. Was it the sun? Or the vision I beheld before my eyes? So slitted and slumped, with biceps that bulged and veins that throbbed and pumped, I saw the light reflecting the New Fiction shelves I'd neglected to scan through before checking out inside. Unable to quell the urge, and undaunted by the less-than-gleeful glances of the library clerks, I two-stepped backward in a Michael Jackson moonwalk shuffle and reentered under the exit sign. Quickly commencing calisthenics, I bent and stretched my strained vertebral column to peruse the surnames sprawled before me across still sturdy and unbroken spines.

Suddenly, one of the novelist's names caught my eye.

Balancing my bundle with a skillfully dexterous maneuver, I slid the book forward and turned it over to read the words "forbidden" and "love" phrased side by side in a blurb on its paperback cover. That look was all it took to persuade me to add the weight of two-hundred and twenty-eight more pages to my leaning tower of prose and boldly take my place back in line.

What happened next amazes me still, and I'm sure it will for all the remaining days of my life. As if I'd been slipped a swig of love potion no. 9, somewhere in the first paragraphs of the novel, I found myself cast under this captivating writer's spell, locked in a trance that lured me to a resourceful site online. With my heart beating wildly in my throat (and other bodily parts keeping time), I entered the Amazonian cyber-jungle and, much to my delight, found several same-authored, previously published works, a few reviews, and most intriguingly, a personal invitation by the hexing and vexing mujer herself, bidding her mesmerized readers to write her.

So I did. And much to my humble and disbelieving, yet paranoid and suspicious surprise, within the hour, a computer-generated guitar (music to my ears) announced the arrival of her even more unexpected reply.

The date = July 2nd = "a date which will live in infamy" = the day we first reached out and e-touched each other = the beginning of a feverishly impassioned correspondence that would forever alter both me and my life. Not only had I connected with a witty, wonderfully gifted, and talented word lover, but also a more than ten-yeared tenured university professor who would, by nature and virtue of her mere professional existence, introduce me to a "field of glorious study" I didn't even know existed at the time. A place where the best of both the English and Spanish worlds peacefully coexist and are harmoniously combined.

But academics aside, we were like two dangling participles and threads at loose ends, longing to be complete sentences in part of a more colorful pattern in the greater woven tapestry of literary life. For this reason, we collaborated upon crossing paths, on written endeavors, arranging and *planning our schedules and lives. No easy feat, considering the great expanse of land between us, more affectionately referred to as our mathematically challenging continental divide.*

Meanwhile, we continued our adventurous and lascivious verbal foray and foreplay via e-voicing our admiration of and appreciation for our mutual, yet distinct, ways with words. By posing aloud ponderings such as, "Does the book—and, by extension, the writer—find its reader? Or the reader of the book its writer?" We lavishly poured on the praise for both published (hers) and unrecognized (mine) abilities and insights.

Looking back over my shoulder with twenty-twenty hindsight, as an eternal and unwavering believer that all things happen for a reason, I remain convinced our roads-less-traveled, which had become dead-end paths, had been out-of-our-worldly-hands meant to intersect. As our bodies, souls, and lives had been destined to celestially intertwine. Beyond that belief, I pragmatically concede realizing that as human beings, we are cruelly prone to misunderstandings and are often pushed or jump off cliffs to plummet headfirst into heartfelt erroneous conclusions in our mere mortal interpretations of the whys. Especially when and where love is in the air, for it is true that the madwoman who free falls does so chutelessly, fumbling around in the dark wearing rose-colored glasses, she is blind. Despite such lucid and apparent rational awareness, from where I sat, as a fervent dreamer at the time, my heart was already on my sleeve, and my head was in the clouds floating high above it. I immediately and unabashedly e-shared with this virtual stranger my thoughts on her literature, my private and personal past, and my peach-faced lovebird's-eye views on the profound perplexities of real life.

What can I say?

It was love at first write.

HEAD-OVER-HEELS, WE MOVED ONTO THE *usual exchanges of photographs (naturally, only those that showed our best sides), then flowers for all-and-no-occasions, with gifts to rival the deliveries of a Kris-Kringling Santa on a certain December night. There were books and jewelry, including a 14K gold* chain, "Because I want you to have and wear something that has touched my skin and caressed the space over my heart and between my breasts," she'd said. I continue to wear it around my neck, although it feels more like a knotted noose now. There was music too. CDs of romantic Latino melodies, some soulful R & B, and Pink's warning shouts.

Questions abounded. Mine (now) were, "What happened? Where did those feelings go?" Hers (then) were, "How can this be? How can I feel so much, so deeply for someone I've yet to meet? Whose voice I've yet to hear? Someone I don't know?" By email, she expressed to me such gnawing concerns as they did a number on her psyche and caused her self-doubt and a mistrust of others. My impulsive and succinctly impetuous reply, a seven-digit number preceded by a three-digit area code.

And so it came to be that one day, short of an exact month from our first contact, our relationship set sail on a course for new waters into unchartered seas as we "let our fingers do the walking" and our voices do the talking, night after night after night. Although my ego-defended memory fails to serve me now in the verbatim recollection of our many multi-hour conversations, a self-proclaimed paradoxical enigma, a timidly aggressive femme on the streets and butch in the sheets, who is loudly outspoken yet quietly shy, I will NEVER forget what I, lustfully and with barely concealed libidinous desires, wantonly whispered before putting the receiver to bed that first hot-and-bothered August night, "Think of me when you touch yourself tonight."

My wish was her command (and vice versa) as we took the advice of the yellow pages' slogan, stocks in AT&T, and we simultaneously soared high. Together, we boldly went where we'd not gone before and promptly plotted to burn the only covered bridges that remained between us by purchasing e-tickets for air travel that would warp speed us through the friendly skies.

We originally agreed to meet in San Antonio. It was, in her well-traveled words, "the most romantic place on the globe." But as the decided-upon September date quickly approached, I frantically fought to stave off the anxious panic of an attack that had me shaking in my size seven-and-a-half scared-to-death shoes. I got cold feet, and my toes froze in petrified fear of what I might (not) find and feel when I would come face to face with the fantasy my overactive heart and vivid imagination had invented and created between the lines.

It wasn't until a springtime West Coast conference that we met in the flesh for the very first time. For her, it was a complete surprise.

After that, we were repeatedly and heatedly—thanks to planes, trains, and automobiles—going between PHX to BWI American Airlines United.

How to describe such indescribable emotions?

A few awkward and wordless (believe it or not) minutes after the big bird's arrival, our souls embraced, our bodies merged. Although I so dislike the expression, we swapped saliva. It was but one more magical moment in the fairy-tale, greatest love ever lived, never-ending story of my life, or so I hopelessly and romantically (mis)believed at the time.

They say all good things must come to an end, and our union was to be no exception to that age-old adage. It would be but a matter of time. And, although no more than four consecutive weeks' worth of circumstances and commitments would keep us geographically separated between rendezvous' during the nineteen chapters/months in the book of our life, it became painfully apparent that as individuals and lovers, we were much more different than we would ever be alike.

In short, she was merlot and linguini with clams. I was a cheeseburger, a Coke, and some fries. She was a dog-loving, stoic admirer of historically educational documentaries. I was a sappy romantic comedy cat person who'd yet to experience the love of a canine with a melancholic penchant for crying my heart out while unashamedly, expressly, and affectionately cuddling on rainy nights. Where it was in my nature to microscopically examine from every angle and perspective, talk to death and overanalyze, she preferred to sweep each and every unspoken speck under the rug, on top of which she demanded we let dozing Dobermans lie. All too aware of our discrepancies, I began to wonder, were we doomed? Or could we be another Gertrude and Alice? Perhaps a Lucy and Ethel? Or would we end up a Jekyll and Hyde?

Many thoughts, concerns, and worries mazed through my muddled mind, but the farthest, most inconceivable (and contrary to "love conquers all") impossibility was that ours was to be but a short story with a not-so-happy ending and no epilogue nor sequel in sight.

Nonetheless, we made it semi-unscathed through those first daunting days to survive the dreaded close encounter with an unexpected and unaware work colleague and the surprise of an ill-timed and misinterpreted vacation call. But when my idea of a relationship as a lifelong, smooth sailing vessel crashed into her anchored, distant, free floating yacht, the waters parted and our relationship (and friendship) began to sink. It was a clear indication we were not on a Love Boat cruise.

"El amor se va." "Love goes away." Those were some of her last words to me as I stared at her incredulously and unblinking, unthinking, my mouth agape and my heart broken wide.

Although she was not my first same-sex-xx-xx-chromosomal love—and in my defense, I had been rubber-rafted to believe that she had drifted in Sapphic waters to the isle of Lesbos herself before,—in light of recent enlightenments, I no longer have a clue what the truth is or was. What does it matter now, anyway?

An astrologically defined Scorpio by birth, I confess I possess all the character traits attributed to my sign. I'm passionate, deep, intense, secretive, jealous, and moody, among other things spelled out on a favorite mega mug of mine. A friend once gave it to me "because scarily you are every one of these things," she said as she hugged, winked, and smiled at me. I drink from it all the time. But where did my shipwrecking marinera read the words in anger she loved to hurl at me, flag-waving, immature, neurotic? Hmm, I'll have to lift the teabag tag and take a closer look next time.

In the end, she said I'd seduced her with words. I often wonder about the meaning of her words. The Oxford dictionary on my desk shows the word defined as, "(to) lead astray, tempt into sin, or crime, corrupt; persuade (person) into abandonment of principles, esp. chastity or allegiance; persuade by temptingness or attractiveness." I remain immortally wounded by such a negation of any love I obviously wrongly believed she ever felt for me. What a low, knockout blow to the depths of a heart's soul, from an opponent who I choose to believe can only live with herself by fabricating such a hurtful lie.

Did she mean to imply that our love was a sin? That a wicked wolf cloaked in a sheep's skin, I'd pulled the itchy wool over her hetero eyes? Had she, pre-me, lived a virginally chaste, vow of celibacy, non-lesbian life?

These are questions for which I will never have answers, since she has repeatedly and completely hung up on me, shut and written me out of her life.

Ironically, and of timely interest, I attended a lecture and discussion given by a privy-to-the-passions-and-privacies-of-my-life longtime friend entitled, "Dramatizing the Obvious: The Writer as Voyeur." Among other fascinations of hers, she brought up a favorite (and coincidental) topic, convinced as she is that "All writing is seduction and all writers seduce when we write."

It is true I unclothe my inner self more freely when hidden behind a sheltering computer screen in private, one-on-one communion with another via my writing. Not in an attempt to "have my way" with my reader/ prey, but because I lack a certain freedom of speech, a non-wower who is not exactly the head-turning type. In the party animal kingdom, I'm much more a shell-shocked and reclusive hermit crab that seeks refuge from the noisy masses that float and flutter by than a gregariously flitting butterfly. Maybe it is because I believe that to really and deeply know and love another, one must dispense with all physical dis- and subtractions first. In my book, there is no match for the powerfully compelling words of a strong-yet-sensitive, tough-yet-tender, nor any candle that can hold a flame that burns more ardently than the chemically arousing, irresistibly combustible fatal attraction to the bare nakedness of a verbosely intelligent and sensuously sensual female writer.

As for whether I will ever "get the lead out" and write another sight unseen again, perhaps it is not for this star-crossed lover to decide the alignment of any future heavenly bodies that may appear, out of the blue, in my Milky Way's galaxy or on my atmospheric horizon. Suffice it to say, it is my unmitigated epistolary belief that "the pen is mightier than the s(poken)word." Thus, if I am to ever do battle on love's field again, my fall *will, in some way, shape, genre, or form, undoubtedly involve a combination of letters and characters brought to life by the more archaic strokes of quills and pens or by the no longer new millennium's constant clicking atop square keys housed in the rectangular shape of an ergonomic board. For such is and will be my inherent and undeniable nature until my internal inkwell drieth up and the writer's lifeblood in me floweth forth no more.*

CHAPTER 14

MENA SMILED AT THE MEMORY of the writing. She contemplated dropping a copy into the package she was putting together to send to Sydney, but ultimately decided against it. She wanted the chain she was returning to be received without any such distractions. If she were to decide to send a message with it, it would not be open to interpretation, but would instead be a straightforward communication.

For the time being, she placed the connected gold links in a padded envelope, put stamps on it, and scheduled its pickup online. She would leave it unsealed until morning, in case she found herself verbally inspired before carrying it to the mailbox. She still hadn't heard from Sydney, and her unexplained disappearance and continued silence were speaking louder than her temporary return had. It seemed like theirs was not just a lost love, but also a lost cause. She knew if she held onto it, she would be holding onto the past and the love for a woman she needed to let go. Breathing a colossal sigh of relief, she felt her life was finally beginning to regain some semblance of control.

That mission accomplished, Mena got back to work. With incident reports piled high around her, she went through the stacks, reading each one carefully in search of patterns, whether in time, place, or response. She started a chart for each fire in a one-hundred-mile radius and recorded the time each was reported, weighing that hour against the time the first firefighter arrived on the scene. It was tedious work with little reward, until she noticed one name seemed to appear much more frequently than others.

Daniel Seth Henderson.

Interesting, she thought, but it didn't prove anything, so she moved on.

However, once she'd marked the dates and times in Sharpie on a huge wall map of the area, she realized the fires were not that far apart. She doubted that anyone would think anything of it unless they'd been looking for trouble. But armed with this information and nearly a dozen old deer cams she had stored in a shed, a plan laid out in her mind.

Using Velcro straps, she'd put the camouflaged digital cameras on trees near the edges of as many surrounding forest roads as numbers would allow, keeping in mind they were both motion activated and very sensitive. Even the wind, if it blew hard enough, would set them off, so she had to choose spots for their placement carefully. Since many tourists visited the area for camping and other recreational activities, she wanted to avoid the most traveled roads while covering the ones the firebug, if there were one, would likely drive down.

She bumped over dirt, spun over gravel, and sailed over asphalt until she'd carefully chosen each spot. Afterward, as she painstakingly reviewed each still capture for weeks on end, one of the things she soon realized was the Coconino wasn't hurting for wildlife.

Joe Peña and Mike Davila stood side by side at the base of what had been Elden Tower and surveyed the damage around them. The fire had burned through the area more than a week before, yet from time to time, hot spots were still being uncovered. That's why they had remained behind, and why they would stay there, until they were convinced it was truly out and over. In his mind, Davila clearly saw the before and after images. He recalled how tall the grass had been on the day they'd found Mena. Every single blade had since been reduced to ash. Amazingly, many of the larger trees, although burned and scarred, still stood. It was a strange but frequent phenomenon in the ponderosa pine forests.

When he first started studying botany and other courses required for a degree in forestry, Davila found a lot of what he had to learn to be boring, worthy only of a snooze session atop a desk at the university. Later in the course of his education, once he was able to get out and about and do some foot- and fieldwork in the lands of the region, he understood the need for what he, as a freshman, had considered useless information.

He was now thankful he had learned how coniferous trees, such as pines, contain an oily substance called resin. How such pitch ignites and burns quickly, allowing fire to pass through fast. And how, because of that, the granddaddies of old growth forests, head and shoulders above the rest and out of reach of a ground fire's flames, stood a good chance of making it out alive. The more substantial the timber, the better the odds. The ponderosa's characteristic thick bark and deep roots also serve to increase their rate of survival, as did the fact that as the trees grow taller, the lower branches fall off, adding to the kindling often found on their forest floors and providing more fuel for a quick burn through. Even though that had been so in this fire too, dead snags—pieces of trees that were not quite as resilient—littered the ground of the decimated land. Like bone fragments in the urn of a recent cremation, they jutted out like tombstones from the ashes.

After more than two full days of mop-up, a process by which the firefighters lined up side by side, dropped to their hands and knees, and literally crawled on the earth to feel for fire seeking refuge underground, spirals of smoke still swirled and danced around. With shovels and flappers, they turned over and under the duff, now mostly soot and ash, and stirred water from five-pound portable containers they carried on their backs into the mix. A dirty and exhausting job, it could sometimes take weeks, depending on how many acres were involved in a burn. This one, although it had its moments, hadn't been quite that bad.

MENA THOUGHT SHE FINALLY HAD the proof she needed in an image captured on one of the camcorders she was monitoring. Unfortunately, it had been too grainy to be of much use. Still, she knew who it was, even without seeing his face. Regardless, she curbed her enthusiasm and prepared for a sojourn in Albuquerque, where she would spend the remaining weeks of her summer vacation. As part of an interagency effort, she'd join forces with men and women from all over the country—from the US Forestry Service, Bureau of Indian Affairs, Bureau of Land Management, the National Park Service, and Fish and Wildlife Services—all of whom were coming together for extensive classroom training and field experience to learn about prescribed fires and fire management at the Southwest Fire Use Training Academy.

She'd had a lot of time to think about and plan the direction of her life's path, which fork in the road she would follow, while recovering from the fall she was now convinced had a purpose for taking place. She had awakened to the reality that she was not as young as she used to be, that it was time for her to think about scaling back. Her recent research into arson investigation had proven to be a consideration. She planned to look into it while there. She was excited about the prospect and couldn't wait.

She'd planned for Peña's wife, Traci, to take care of Chesa and Emi while she was gone, though she hated the thought of leaving them again so soon and for so long.

"WHAT EXACTLY DID YOU THINK would happen? Better yet, what did you want to happen?" Liz asked Sydney, who had just spent the better half of fifty minutes outlining her journey to Arizona while anxiously pacing around the room. Liz couldn't recall ever having seen or heard her so agitated as she listened to Sydney recount in detail each word of every conversation that had taken place, from the telephone call that had alerted her to Mena's life-threatening situation to the hospital visit.

"Well…I guess I wanted her to be happy to see me." Sydney sighed sadly. "Truth be known, a part of me has always held onto the fantasy that someday we would get back together. I believed what we had was special, that it didn't come along every day. But then, what did I know? I'm not exactly a paragon of any kind of relationship or love guru. I often wondered what would happen if and when our paths would cross again. The reality of what happened, however, was far different than anything I'd ever considered in my wildest imagination. I guess I was fooling myself to think she still cared."

Liz stopped her monologue there. "You *did* share some precious times together, and I'm sure she does still care. Maybe just not in the way you had hoped she would. Correct me if I'm wrong, but for months, didn't she try to reach out to you by way of calls and letters? I have a somewhat vague memory of you reading and sharing quite a few of them with me in our sessions. Isn't it possible that she, like you, had to find a way to distance herself from the pain of ending the relationship? I doubt seriously that she ever expected to see you again. She must have been shocked by the unexpected appearance of her past in the present."

Sydney unsnapped her purse and pulled out the chain Mena had returned. "This arrived in the mail this morning."

Liz's eyes widened, then her forehead creased. "I don't understand. Are you telling me that Mena has sent you a gift?"

Sydney explained, "I gave this chain to her after removing it from around my own neck the first time we made love."

"Oh. I see."

"I didn't want it back. I'd given it to her. She'd kept it all this time, apparently worn it as recently as the day of the accident." Sydney struggled not to lose control of her emotions as she attempted to recount the experience.

"It's hard to let go of someone we've loved. Especially someone we have loved as much as you loved Mena. It would be difficult if she had been taken from this world by death, but in its own way, perhaps it's better to have thought that you still had a chance then to now know that may never be so, by her choice."

In her own way, Liz validated what the grieving woman was feeling. As she continued to watch her fight for control over her emotions, Liz asked a point-blank question. "Sydney, why don't you just let yourself cry? You know, it really is okay. What do you think would happen if you simply let the tears fall? Would that be such a terrible thing?"

Sydney laughed, a reactionary response, before revealing one of her greatest fears. "They might never stop coming." Over the years, she had acquired and honed coping skills and strategies in response to earlier trauma that she still used today. In an environment that had been, for a while, out of her control, she found solace and felt safe when she was able to maintain some semblance of dominion in the face of a threatening foe. It had become her way of surviving.

These days, she rarely admitted the truth, opting instead to tout the virtues of an adopted stoicism as a preferred and more acceptable character trait. Unfortunately, it was more a character flaw, a crumbling facade, a charade.

Sydney continued to choke back a sob as she put the necklace back in its place, and Liz asked, "So, where do you go from here?"

"I don't really know."

Such a response from a woman who planned absolutely everything, and had often insisted that to do otherwise, "Like a fish out of water, I would flounder," surprised not only Liz, but even Sydney herself.

"Please think about it. Our time today is just about up, but we'll make that the focus of next week's session."

As they walked down the stairs to the center's front door, Liz turned to her. "I understand how difficult this must be for you. Just know I'm here for you and will make time if you need to come in before next week."

Sydney nodded. "Thank you."

"And remember, no matter the outcome, you reached out. You'll be fine. Just keep your chin up."

As the door closed behind her, Sydney heard Liz greet her next client and thought, *That's easy for you to say,* before stepping down off the porch.

THAT EVENING, WHEN NIGHT FELL and she was again set adrift on a sea of profound aloneness, Sydney reflected on what she *didn't* say to Liz. *Why didn't I tell her that I hadn't returned to see Mena as promised?*

Did I try as hard as I could have to reach her? Couldn't I have delayed my return flight just one more day? Mena would have stopped at nothing if the roles had been reversed. I know it. But I'm not her. Surely, she'll understand when I finally tell her what happened, won't she? Or am I simply falling back into my old ways? Have I really changed?

She reread the words Mena had written and sent along with the chain.

I've heard it said that people come into our lives for a reason, a season, or a lifetime. Sometimes we get confused about which it is, sometimes the three overlap, but in the end, I think the theory holds true. Sydney, we had a reason, and a very good season. We both have memories to cherish that will last a lifetime, but somewhere along the way, we stepped into a Robert Frost poem. You know, the one about the road not taken. We could have gone either way, but a decision had been made, and it was made by you. Not that I'm casting blame. Our paths diverged by way of so many winding bends and turns that, after a while, even if we had wanted to, we couldn't go back to where we'd parted ways. We're different people now. We've both been affected and changed by experiences we've had along our separate paths. Even if we could find our way back, it wouldn't be the same. You're not the same, and I'm not the same, and together, we surely wouldn't be the same. Of course, maybe that wouldn't be such a bad thing.

Sydney paused for a moment and reflected. She imagined the dimpled smile that would appear on Mena's face if she were saying these words to her right now in this space.

I meant each and every (what you referred to as sappy) word I wrote in my many, many letters, emails, and cards. And I don't regret telling you how I felt. I will always be grateful for the time we had together. Ours was a magical love. But I've come to realize that the romance and fantasy is not enough. We could never survive the ups and downs of everyday life. Like someone special once said to me, 'we simply weren't meant to be,' but if you keep your heart open, don't give up, and believe, you'll find your soul's mate, someone else to love.

The note had been handwritten and tied with a ribbon around the small box into which Mena had carefully coiled the chain. Sydney thought she knew what was inside even before she'd lifted the lid and separated the cotton to see. However, no amount of forewarning had prepared her for the torrent of emotion that gripped her heart or the deluge of tears that came.

Sydney had no words for what she felt, maybe because it was a cathartic numbing. Paralleling Mena's fateful departure on that decisive winter day, Sydney looked at the necklace and felt her heart breaking. Suddenly, she felt inspired by the awareness that Mena had also worn the chain. And, by putting it back around her neck, in a way, she'd be keeping her close, as she had suggested when she first gave it to Mena.

As if it were instilled with magic, she knew what she had to do.

AT THE END OF AUGUST, Mena was back home in Yuma, proudly wearing her newly earned patch depicting a lightning bolt embroidered in the center of a bear paw on the sleeve of her jacket. The outer design represented power and leadership, the fearlessness required to stave off panic and unwise decision-making, necessary when fighting fire. The inner stitching, a sign of natural ignition, symbolized their power and control over fire management.

Her life began to settle back into its former routine. Thus, she began to pack away her fire gear and get out her school supplies, put aside fire analysis papers and put together lesson plans.

On a Saturday morning that found her knee-deep in such a mess, she was surprised by a knock at the door. Chesa started barking excitedly, and Emi seized the opportunity of the distraction to bat wadded-up balls of discarded notebook paper back and forth across the living room floor. In the time it took Mena to disengage herself from the boxes and textbooks she'd been perusing and that had piled all over the floor, the solicitor or visitor had found the bell and was now laying on it hard.

"I'm coming, I'm coming! Hold your horses!"

"Hold my horses?" Mena heard repeated from the other side of the door. She smiled at the recognition of a familiar voice.

"Well…hello, stranger." Mena managed while stumbling across the threshold and nearly knocking Isa off the porch.

"It's so good to see you, Mena." Isa greeted and hugged her friend. "It's been a long time. How've you been?"

"I'm hanging. Although, by the looks of it…" she gestured around, "the thread is fraying." Using her foot, Mena pushed the books and papers to the side and invited Isa in. "What brings you here?" she asked.

"I wanted to visit my family, spend a few days with them before the semester starts."

"Oh, yeah, I forgot. You're in school, too."

Isa laughed as she looked around and surveyed the damage on the floor. "So this is how teachers plan for classes, is it? I often wondered."

"Well, I'm pretty sure most are more organized than this." Mena laughed. "Have a seat on the sofa. Let me grab a few beers and a bowl of chips. I'll be right back."

While she was gone, Isa happened to look down at what she assumed was a discard pile. On top of it, the title of what appeared to be a short story caught her eye. But before she could reach for it, Mena returned.

"So, what's new?" Mena crunched around one of the salty triangular treats, sat back for a rest, and waited to be filled in.

Isa told her all about the last days of the fire and what she knew about the rest of the crew before saying, "Guess what?" But when a shrug of the shoulders was all she received, Isa blurted out the news that she'd been dating Mike Davila. "You know Mike?"

Mena pursed her lips, and a crease appeared between her eyebrows. "Mike, about 5'10", dark hair, mustache, real cute."

"Actually, I wouldn't have noticed. Wait a minute." She thought she remembered the name, and she asked, "The guy who found me?"

"…and carried you up that steep slope. Uh-huh. That's him. He saved your life, you know."

"And you fell for him because you suffer from a hero's or savior's complex?"

"Oh, don't even go there."

Both women laughed, then Mena—who they'd all thought had been home, taking it easy and recovering—told her about her stint at the academy and about how she was playing catch-up to transition to the role of teacher from student these days.

"What's that?" Isa pointed to the short story she'd seen earlier.

Mena looked to see what she meant. "It's nothing. A story I wrote a long time ago."

"I love the title. It sounds interesting. Do you mind if I read it?"

Mena considered the ramifications for a moment before deciding, "Sure, go ahead. I was just going to throw it out."

Isa pulled it onto her lap and changed the subject, "So tell me, what have you got planned for your kids this year? What will you be teaching? Any exciting, new stuff?"

"I guess that remains to be seen." Mena responded. "You know, I'm still trying to get used to coming at language from the other side. I mean, I started out helping Spanish-speaking kids with English so they could get by with their other classes in school, then I taught Spanish to kids so far removed from the border that they didn't know where Mexico was. Now, here I am, practically sitting in Mexico, where there's a huge need to teach Spanish to a generation whose families speak it at home, but they don't understand all of what's being said. That would be my guess, but we haven't received our assignments yet." She stooped to pick one of the picture books up. "I've missed reading to the younger kids and sharing with them about Hispanic and Latino culture. They loved this book." She opened it and flipped through the colorful pages.

Even though Isa hadn't asked, Mena, caught up in the memory, offered a synopsis, "It's about a little girl, the daughter of migrant workers. The only thing she wants is a place to call home, to stop moving around so much, so she can make friends at school. You wouldn't believe how quiet and still those kids could be when I'd read. They loved it. It would amaze me. I liked to use the stories to help build their vocabulary, that way they were learning culture and language at the same time. I think, I hope, it made learning for them more interesting. Teaching that way was fun for me." She smiled, put the book in one of the boxes, and stayed silent for a moment, thinking.

Until Isa asked, "Why don't you just call her?"

As fate would have it, at that precise moment, the phone rang.

Mena raised both eyebrows to her hairline, hunched her shoulders, and cocked her head in mock wonderment before picking it up.

"Hello."

There was no answer for a minute, but just when Mena was about to hang up, she heard another voice she recognized at the line's other end.

"You haven't been out fighting fires again, have you?"

Mena looked at Isa, her eyes wide open in surprise, before laughing. "No. Doctor's orders forbade it for the rest of the season, which is almost over now, anyway. At least, it is for me. How's it going, Alex?"

"Busted, I am. I was just organizing and moving around some files here at work when I put my hand on yours and thought I'd risk a firing offense by calling to see how you're doing." Both women laughed before Alex said, "Anyway, I'm glad to hear you're taking it a little easier these days. I don't know how you do what you do. It's such a risky occupation."

Mena couldn't resist. "Yeah, I know what you mean. Some of those eighth graders, especially, under the influence of raging hormones, *can* be pretty scary."

"Yes, they can. Wait. I'm sorry. What? What are you talking about? What did you say?"

"Alex, fighting fires is only a summer job for me. I teach school for a living. Call me crazy, but I love kids and learning and teaching, watching their faces light up. I especially love the little ones when I read them stories or help them create a work of art that bridges two worlds and promotes an understanding of differences. For our last project of the year, we used yarn and glue to make Eyes of God, and I must admit to a certain amount of pride in the discussions that came out of their weaving, not to mention their beautiful handcrafted creations."

"I had no idea. I thought you were a professional firefighter."

"I am. It's just not all that I do."

As if suddenly remembering Isa was there, Mena said, "Alex, I'm sorry I can't talk for too long, I have company. Isa's here with me, but there is something I wanted to ask, so you have perfect timing. I'm gonna need to revisit the scene of the crime one of these days, and I was wondering if you could recommend a hotel, a place to stay."

"Here in Flagstaff, I presume?"

"Yep, that's close enough."

Alex hesitated only for a moment. "You're more than welcome to stay here with me."

"Alex, I really wasn't fishing for an invitation."

"I didn't think you were, but I have plenty of unoccupied space. As a matter of fact, I've considered turning my place into a bed and breakfast. I could experiment with you as a guest." She laughed. "And, of course, Isa is welcome too. The more the merrier. Bring her along."

Warming to the idea, Mena admitted, "That sounds great. If you're sure you don't mind? And it wouldn't be too much of an imposition."

"Not at all. I'll look forward to it, and to introducing you to the love of my life, my daughter, Kimberly."

CHAPTER 15

SYDNEY ROSE BEFORE THE SUN made an appearance on the horizon the next morning. The hopefulness she was beginning to feel instead of helplessness that had been weighing upon her so heavily was already instilling her with boundless energy. She had hardly slept at all.

After a quick cup of coffee, she gathered her books and papers, secured her laptop in its bag, and headed for the university, making a beeline for Epstein's office.

"SYDNEY, GOOD MORNING. I WAS surprised to see your appointment on my calendar. What brings you here? Come on in." Stephen Epstein, Academic Dean at UMD, smiled and ushered her past him into his workday domain. "Have a seat. Make yourself cozy. Can I offer you a cup of coffee?"

"No, thank you. I've already had three."

He moved to the Keurig on the credenza where he prepared one for himself before sliding into his seat, bracing himself for what was coming. "What is it that has you so worried and nervous? Or is that just the caffeine?"

"Something very unexpected has come up. A personal matter that I'm afraid might take a while to resolve. I think I might need an earlier out than originally planned."

"You're scaring me, Sydney. Are you talking a sabbatical? How much time? Starting when?"

"Don't worry, Stephen. I should be able to finish the fall semester out, but I hope to have everything wrapped up here before Christmas." Sydney hated to do this to the man. He'd been so good to her over the years. Instrumental in her promotions. Supporting her research, travels, and endeavors. He'd been a good friend. And, while she knew she wasn't irreplaceable, the first semester of the year would be starting in just a few weeks, and as a department chair, she wasn't sure how loud the clamoring would be to take over her position. She wished she could give him more notice.

"I'm sure Elena will cover for a while, regardless of when I leave. She's been interested in the position for some time now, and I think she'd appreciate the chance to get a feel for what's involved with it. It would give you a chance to see how she'd do before either of you would have to make a permanent commitment. That should also give you enough time to search for an appropriate candidate"

"I just don't know what to say, Sydney. I must admit, I'm a little shocked. I had no idea this was coming. It sounds like you're talking an early retirement. Are you? Has UCLA finally convinced you to pull up stakes?"

With a sly smile, Sydney slid an envelope containing her letter of resignation across the desk.

He opened it, and as he read, he peered over the top of his glasses. "So this is it, huh? Our days together are now numbered. Do you mind if I ask where you're going?"

"Arizona."

"Are you *kidding* me? Who the hell goes to Arizona? I thought you enjoyed the winters here, the cold weather. You sure won't see any snow in that godforsaken hotter than hell place?"

Sydney laughed. "Come now, Stephen. Surely you know it snows in the northern part of the state, where I'm currently looking to relocate."

"Regardless, I'm sure you must have a good reason. And, in all seriousness, you've done us a great service here for many years. I just hope you're here long enough for a hell of a send-off. We owe you that much, at least."

"Thank you, Stephen. I'll keep you posted."

"And Sydney, if it really can't wait and you need to leave sooner, we'll manage. Do what you need to do. It'll be okay."

"Thanks again, Stephen. I've been blessed to have such a good man as you as my dean."

"Señorita Mendoza, can we sing the song today?"

"Hoy no, mi'jo, tal vez mañana. Not today, sweetie, maybe tomorrow."

"¿Pero, por qué? But why?"

"No tenemos tiempo. We don't have time."

"Pero tenemos casi media hora. But we have almost half an hour."

"Sí, pero tenemos algo nuevo para aprender hoy. Yes, but we have something new to learn today."

Much to Mena's delight, she was taken out of the ESL program and returned to teaching Spanish full-time. The children, equally exuberant in their desire to jump back into the language they loved learning with a teacher who made doing so fun in class, wanted to sing the body parts song, but having already proven rhyme had enabled them to retain the words for face, head, hands, feet, mouth, teeth, eyes, ears, and nose, they were about to move on to the next chapter: articles of clothing.

This time, in lieu of melody, they were going to combine words with action. Mena had strung a rope across the middle of the classroom, and on the floor beside it there was a basket full of clothes and a bag of wooden pins. Today was wash day; they'd be doing laundry, hanging clothes, colgando ropa, and continuing to prove that efforts to think outside of the book would make all the difference in learning.

When Mena had first started teaching, she was overwhelmed by the amount of planning and preparation involved. She'd had no idea how much work went on at home by educators after the last bell. But then, she had been hired by a private school with limited funds and was expected to teach various levels of the language to children with different acquisition abilities, ranging from the ages of five to thirteen. While the little ones loved reading and games, the older ones were a bit more of a challenge. The eighth graders were prone to boredom and far from fans of it, keeping her on her toes and always thinking of ways to reach and inspire them. By her second year, after having made it through probation, she felt substantially more confident. These days, she thrived on the energy that went into constantly revising and revamping her curriculum.

"I want you to think way back, to the end of last May," Mena closed up the day's lesson, "to when we learned about the Spanish explorer, Hernán Cortés, and the Conquest of México. We read an interesting story about an Aztec princess who lived in the land now called Mexico City, then called…what?" she prompted.

Several of her students responded, "Teotihuacán!" Mena looked pleased they had remembered.

"What do you remember about the story? Do you remember the woman's name?" Mena went to the board, picked up a marker, and began her infamous failings at artistic creations by scribbling stick people and what were supposed to be geographical illustrations.

"So here we have…"

"The United States."

"En español, por favor. In Spanish, please."

"Los Estados Unidos."

"Let's practice our directional words…and *under* los Estados Unidos…"

"Detrás de…" one of them guessed incorrectly.

"Nice try, but…" Mena shook her head.

"Adelante de …" someone else shouted out.

"Tampoco. That's not it either. I can see we're going to have to review more than history."

Groans in anticipation of a grammatical review filled the room. It was Rachel who, by process of elimination, came up with the right translation, "Debajo de…"

"Eso es. That's it, pero, en frase completa. A complete sentence, por favor."

"México es el país debajo de los Estados Unidos."

"Muy bien. Very good." Mexico is the country under the United States on my map. Careful now…" She joked playfully, daring them to mock her drawing, lest they pay the consequence of having more than one essay question to answer this time.

Glancing at the clock, Mena saw that there were only five minutes left before the class would end. "Bueno, clase, se nos acabó el tiempo. Voy a poner su tarea en la pizarra. Quiero que repasen la historia de la conquista de México. Se encuentra en las páginas once y doce." She pointed to the book and reminded them to study pages eleven and twelve, where they'd find the history of the conquest of Mexico. "Y no se olviden que mañana hay prueba."

The class grumbled at the reminder that tomorrow, there would be a test.

"We're all products of our pasts. It's important, muy importante, that we don't forget it. Hasta mañana. Qué les vaya bien."

"Adiós, Señorita Mendoza."

As the children picked up their books and backpacks and headed out the door, Mena gathered her own things and tidied up, starting by erasing the board. It had been a long day. She was glad tomorrow was Friday, even though it was also the end of the marking period, which meant she'd have many papers to grade over the weekend, to somehow squeeze into her already overfull agenda. Thank God it would be a long one. She decided to get as much done as she could Friday night and started off as soon as she got home by readying her ride. Isa was invited to spend the night. She'd become a good friend, and Mena no longer felt as awkward around her, especially now that she was seeing Mike.

She hooked up the hose, went into the garage in search of a bucket, and grabbed a sponge on her way out. It had been a while since she'd given the Jeep a good cleaning, so she worked her way from the inside out. With most of the windows open in the house, she tested her lung capacity by shouting, "Alexa, play Enrique Iglesias." Given the device's song selection, Mena thought, *Alexa must have been kicked to the curb a time or two herself.*

With impeccable timing, Isa pulled up as "El Perdedor" came on.

"Oh, no! Isa quickly exclaimed. "We can't be having this. Mujer, it's time to move on from these depressing songs."

"What are you talking about? This song is so beautiful."

Isa looked at her with her head tilted down and her eyes rolled up.

"Okay, it might be sad, but it's still beautiful. Don't you know that sad songs say so much?" Mena realized if she continued to quote "Rocket Man," she'd soon have royalties to cough up. She laughed. Isa was the best at lifting her spirits. She was starting to feel like her old self.

"Well, if you insist on listening to Kiké, at least pick a tune with a little more bounce." She looked around for the source of the sound and realized it was coming from inside the house.

"Just tell me what you want."

"Bailando."

"Alexa, play 'Bailando' by Enrique Iglesias."

As the song began, Isa said, "That's much better."

Mena had to admit, music had a certain sorcery about it. Just a few beats in, and her mood was lightening up.

"We could call this *Carwash Karaoke*. James Corden, eat your heart out." Isa laughed as she moved to beat on the brim of Mena's ball cap, danced and sang her way over to the bucket, and pulled out the soapy sponge before throwing it across the Jeep's hood and hitting Mena with it, right on target. Naturally, Mena's instinct had her retaliate by way of turning the hose onto her assailant. Just like that, they were ensconced in a water war.

AFTER THEY'D FINISHED WASHING THE Jeep, putting everything back in its place, and exhausted from all the playful maneuvers, they went inside and ordered a pizza. While awaiting its arrival, they took turns showering and finished just as it was being delivered.

Mena brought two beers out and saw Isa was already working on her second slice. "It must be nice to be young," she sighed.

Isa smirked. "You know, you never told me about you and Sydney. She told me a little of your story while we were hanging out waiting for you to wake up, but, as you know, there's two sides to every story, and the truth usually lies somewhere in the middle."

Mena looked at her with a quizzical smile. "Do you really expect me to believe you haven't read my short story yet? I know you better than that."

Isa pulled her hat down over her eyes.

"I thought so, so there's nothing else to know."

PACKED UP, OUT THE DOOR, and on their way, Mena handed over the printout of the MapQuest directions to her navigator, who was already snoring loudly in the passenger seat.

Mena knew just how to wake her. She slid Gloria Trevi's CD into the player and advanced it to her version of "Como yo te amo." She didn't have to wait long.

The intro had barely given way to the singer's emoting when Isa began to stir, wrinkling her nose and brow. "Oh, no. No way. Where do you come up with this stuff?" She twisted around in the seat and reached for her backpack. Pulling it into her lap, she unzipped the front compartment, quickly ejected the CD, then pushed in her replacement.

Mena teased, "Oh, come on. The violins, the cello, even. I just don't understand where you get your music appreciation."

Isa looked at her and said, "Really." She shook her head. "Well, not from the depths of a dark depression, obviously. But I was ready for you this time. I knew what was coming. Now, this one, it's a love song, just of a different nature." She winked at Mena. "And I don't want to hear any objections from the driver either." She sat back in her seat as Rihanna sang "Te Amo."

Mena had to admit—to herself, if not to Isa—the song was catchy. She soon began bopping her head to the beat.

"And what is this?" Isa motioned to the maps Mena had piled in her lap while she was sleeping. "I mean, who does this?"

"Uh, people who need to know where they're going."

"Are you kidding me?" Isa tossed the papers onto the floorboard and asked, "Siri, how do I get to..." She reached down for the page on top to look for the address again before continuing.

Music helped make the drive time more enjoyable. The banter between the two women also helped immensely as they whiled away time, promoting and debating different songs and singers until they reached their destination.

"Are you sure this is it?" Isa asked. "I thought she said it was a cabin."

"She did, and it is, just not like the Lincoln Logs that we imagined."

"This place is ginormous."

Mena pulled up the driveway and beeped, not wanting to make it all the way to the door before Alex knew they'd arrived. But she needn't have bothered; both Alex, and a girl who looked to be about seven or eight and she assumed was Kim, were there to greet their visitors before the sound of the Jeep's horn had completely dissipated.

Alex hugged her, then turned to Isa with the same affectionate welcome before introducing her daughter. "Kimmy, I'd like you to meet some friends of mine, the ones I told you about. This is Isa, and that's Mena."

Isa went up to her and said, "Your mother told me lots of things about you, young lady. I know all your secrets. Like how ticklish you are." She lunged for the girl's sides and moved her fingers lightly like a butterfly over her hip area, eliciting shrieks of delight. They became fast friends after that introduction.

Once inside, both women marveled at how, if it were possible, the house was even more gorgeous within. The planks of flawlessly shellacked pine making up the floor had obviously been carefully chosen to match the similarly stained knotty cabinets that added a splash of lighter color in the luxury of a wide-open space. With cathedral ceilings that rose to open beams that matched the rest of the woodwork and walls that complemented their golden tones in contrasting hues of colonial blues, burnt oranges, rustic reds, greens, and grays, the next thing they noticed was the breathtaking view. Both the backyard woods and the mountain peaks in the distance, were visible on all sides by way of floor-to-ceiling glass walls that let in lots of natural light. If that weren't enough, the place looked like it could easily grace the cover of any home interior magazine. It was elegantly, yet comfortably decorated, artistically adorned, and immaculately clean.

Feeling slightly insecure upon looking around and making mental comparisons between her humble abode and this dynamic dwelling, Mena unbelievably and doubtingly asked, "Are you sure it's okay that I brought Chesa and Emi along?"

"Are you kidding? They're part of the family. I wouldn't expect you to leave them behind." Both women smiled, and Kimmy beamed. It didn't take the girl long to fall in love with both animals, and as the children, two- and four-legged, escaped down the hall to where they could romp and play, Alex showed Isa and Mena to their rooms and walked them through the rest of the spacious place.

"Your home is beautiful, Alex," Mena said. "Are you sure you want to allow strangers inside to mess it up?"

Alex bit her nail. "Well, I would be here to keep an eye on them. I said a B and B, not a Vrbo."

"Even worse!" Isa chimed in. "Haven't you seen 'The Shining?' or 'Pacific Heights?'"

Mena tried to silence her, but she was on a title-dropping cinema roll.

"Just keeping it real," she said.

"To tell you the truth," Mena broke in, "although I wouldn't be quite as theatrical as Isa in my dissuasion, I'd be afraid these days, Alex. Especially with Kim around."

"Oh, I wouldn't dream of having people stay when she was here. But if your goal was to give me second thoughts, you've achieved it. Maybe I'll limit my guests to friends and those they can vouch for."

Back in the kitchen area, they took seats at the bar while Mena and Isa shared their plans for the weekend with Alex, who listened attentively and appeared intrigued. After coming to the consensus that it'd be best to wait until tomorrow to begin the working part of their vacation, their thoughts turned to play.

Calling Kimmy down from where she'd ultimately retreated to, the four humans sat down at the dining room table for a round of board games. *Life* was the first they set out.

"It's been so long since I played this," Mena said. "I can't wait." When the time came for Kim to marry in the game, and she, of her own accord, chose another pink peg for her plastic car's passenger seat, Alex raised an eyebrow at Mena, but neither of them said a word, nor did they give any indication that they'd seen anything out of the ordinary.

Sometime later, after having given up on their collective dreams of ever making it to Millionaire Estates, the quartet settled for early retirement, counted their money, and put Milton Bradley's source of entertainment away. Then, bored with the games, they retreated to the living space, where it was Isa's turn for a surprise. She'd brought along DVDs they could all watch together, as friends and a family.

"Let's see. What'd you get?" an excited Kim asked as she reached for the cased films.

"Well, since I really had no way of both surprising you and knowing what you'd already seen or might like, I took a chance with my selection. Just keep that in mind." Isa handed the movies to Kim while looking over the girl's shoulder at her mother, who appeared genuinely pleased.

"Wow! I can't believe it. I've been waiting for this one." Kim squealed with delight when she saw the cover of the *Freaky Friday* remake. "Can we watch it? Can we please?" she pleaded before having even seen the other two titles. They never saw the light of day once Kim had decided which it would be.

"Well," Alex exclaimed. "It looks like you've outdone yourself, Ms. Salas." She got up from the sofa and went to the kitchen to pop some corn for them to enjoy while they watched the movie.

At bedtime, Kim—again, of her own accord—sought both visitors out to give them a hug and wish them a good night while dropping hints and suggestions for what tomorrow might bring.

THE NEXT MORNING, WITH ALEX and Kim along, Mena and Isa set out for the roads around Elden Tower. There, they mapped out and set up cameras, checking for any debris that might tell a story. When their work was done, they had some time for a little fun.

In the evening, although they were all tired and dragging from the day's walking and hiking, Kim discovered Isa, especially, was still a willing and formidable opponent in the world of pillow fights.

The three-day getaway flew by as holiday weekends often do. With her Jeep packed up and ready to go, Mena turned to Alex and said, "Thank you so much for inviting us to your home."

Isa followed close behind with, "Let me know when you make up your mind about hosting guests, and I'll talk up your place to everyone I know, if I know they wouldn't be an Anthony Perkins kinda psycho."

"Get out of here, you!" Alex gently pushed her out of their hug and couldn't help but laugh.

CHAPTER 16

As FATE AND COINCIDENCE WOULD have it, at the same time, Sydney was also packing for a trip that would bring her close to where Mena was about to pass through. She knew because Isa had, thankfully, reached out to her at the university again. When Sydney told her what happened and why she hadn't called, Isa was tempted to give her Mena's number, but she wasn't yet sure it was in her best interest. She needed a little more convincing. And soon, Sydney would provide it.

While sipping her coffee, she was curious to know what Isa would even say if she'd been aware of Sydney's pending journey, without knowing the details and its purpose.

She was about to take the biggest leap of faith she'd ever considered in all her life's five decades. And, while she felt she was ready to retire and could write from pretty much anywhere, she'd never dreamed she'd be one day doing so in the Grand Canyon state.

After much careful consideration, she'd settled on Sedona in her search for real estate. Once that had been decided, it was only a matter of hours of searching online listings before she found one that caught her eye and held her attention. It called to her each time she dared look at another place. With custom wrought iron gates that opened onto a beautiful, bricked drive and gorgeous red rock view, she was sold before she even took a virtual glimpse inside. She picked up the phone to call the agent.

"This one will go fast," the realtor said. "It just went on the market yesterday, and I've already had several inquiries."

With an asking price over eight hundred thousand, it was a little expensive, but this would be the last house she'd ever buy—regardless of what happened, if anything, with her and Mena. So without further ado and any hesitation, she made an appointment to see it Saturday. Those charming cherry floors, the stone fireplace wall with niches, and the exposed beams of a soaring ceiling... Even the street's name, Broken Arrow Vista, was all so perfect. She'd say a prayer and keep her fingers crossed, believing that if it was meant to be, the pieces would all fall into place.

FINALLY, SHOWTIME ARRIVED. SHE TUNED out the running commentary of the dapper salesman the minute she'd stepped foot inside the brick-and-mortar house and realized the photographs hadn't done justice to the interior space. This was it. She knew it, she could feel it. Even more strongly than she had with the purchase of her current dwelling place. It was all she could do to keep from pulling out her checkbook before the tour had ended. *So much for not appearing like an overly anxious prey.* Had it been offered, she would have bought it with all of the furnishings and saved herself the hassle of moving all but her personal belongings. Whoever lived there had exquisite taste. Every piece of furniture, wall art, and decoration appeared to have been custom designed for where it sat, hung, or was arranged.

Sydney asked fearfully, "Will a one-hundred-thousand-dollar deposit be enough to keep any other interested party from snatching it away from me?"

The man smiled. "I'm sure that amount of an earnest offering will show the seller you're entering the transaction in good faith." The man was likely already calculating his commission as he pulled out a precontract, and her signature was obtained, along with the check.

Sydney spent the rest of the weekend exploring what would soon be her new town. Her first stop was at what appeared to be a divine French restaurant, René at Tlaquepaque. After quite a delectable deliberation, she ordered the cedar plank salmon and paired it with the suggested and celebratory pinot noir.

Cheers to my new life! She raised her glass in a toast to whatever was to come her way. All during the meal, her thoughts drifted to include Mena. She knew she should have let her know her plans, but the truth was she was afraid. Afraid to be dissuaded. Afraid to find out Mena had given up on her, on their love. Afraid of so many things.

Afterward, she strolled the streets of the neighboring arts enclave, finding herself in awe and admiration of what she found, already mentally decorating. When her legs grew weary of walking and the sky gave way to darker hues, she returned to the rental car and decided to call it a successful day.

She'd only traveled a few miles when she happened upon the Chapel of the Holy Cross, a modern architectural structure built into the buttes in such a way that she almost hadn't recognized it for what it was, until light reflecting from the setting sun drew her attention to the rood that comprised the building's front centerpiece. At first glance, it looked more like an observatory, perched high on a roadside hilltop, but as she drew near, she saw it for the place of worship it was.

You can take the girl out of the church, but the church will always be in the girl.

The first thing she noticed as she entered the building was the life-size, bronze "Christ of the Holy Cross," a piece that had been commissioned and created locally. The artist, she read, chose to show Jesus crucified upon the Tree of Life. There was much symbolism and intricate meaning crafted into the sculptor's work. Sydney purchased and lit a votive, then kneeled to have a few long overdue words with her Lord and Savior.

As she rose and turned to leave, her eyes cast upon a painting titled *Our Lady of Mercy* and four silk hangings known collectively as God's Mercy. She could have gazed at the pieces for hours. It was sure to be a place to which she would not only return, but would visit often.

On Sunday, she had a few morning hours before her flight was scheduled to depart, so she set off early for Doe Mountain, where she was told she'd have her best chance of seeing the sun's magnificent rise on exquisite display. And, she had to admit, she agreed with whomever had given her that insider information. Trite as it seemed, it was stunning. But already thinking of the place as home, perhaps she was biased. She hated to leave, but she found solace in knowing the sooner she finished wrapping things up back east, she'd be returning here to live out the rest of her sunrises and days of her life.

THANKSGIVING HAD ALWAYS BEEN A special holiday for Sydney. She preferred it over the hustling and bustling, gift-giving commercialism Christmas had become. It was a time of giving thanks, of appreciating the blessings life had put in your path and rained down from above, like the golden autumn leaves that still surrounded her.

She turned to the patio door as it slid open.

"It seems so strange to be here," Isa commented. She had gone back inside to trade in her lightweight jacket for a warmer coat. The pleasant temperature of the day had quickly given way to a colder-than-expected early evening.

Sydney smiled. It was November, sweater weather, her favorite time of year. There was a good enough chill in the air that you had to layer, never knowing what winds would blow your way or how cold the deceptively bright day might become in an instant of cloud cover or after the setting sun.

"I'm glad you came. I enjoy having guests. I don't do it nearly as much as I should. Don't get me wrong, I like my alone time too. But it's nice every now and again to have some company, to hear a voice in the house other than the television newscasters or meteorologists who spend time with me regularly."

Jenny took that as her cue to rouse herself from her resting spot and remind her human she could always be depended on to be around.

"Of course, you will be here, girl. You always are. I was referring more to the two-legged variety of living creatures, those that can do a little more than bark and whine. But I do love you so." She kissed the sheltie on her muzzle.

Appeased with that display of affection, the dog went back over to the corner of the deck, circled a few times in search of the best spot, and curled up.

"I guess what I was trying to say is that I feel a bit odd being here. I mean, because of Mena. It's like I'm doing something behind her back, somehow betraying her, our friendship and trust. She has no idea you and I have been in touch, and I'm not sure she'd be happy if she were to find out." Isa opened her arms in a gesture encompassing her present environment.

"Nonsense," Sydney replied, effectively rerouting the subject. "Besides, she has no need to ever know. We're merely two friends spending time together, and as long as we're not slandering her or involving her, why should she care? Your boyfriend has gone home to be with his family, and you'll soon be joining yours back in Arizona. You merely accepted an irresistible invitation to spend a few days in a place you've never seen or visited before, one to which many people flock during vacations and holidays. This area is a mecca for tourists.

"There's so much to see and do, to experience. History and culture, man-made and natural beauty, all within a day's reach. From where you're sitting at this very moment, an hour's drive south will put you in the heart of our nation's capital. The architecture of the buildings and monuments alone is absolutely stunning, gorgeous.

"A half-hour to the north, and you'll be in the middle of Gettysburg's Battlefield, a Civil War lover's dream spot, and just a short drive past picturesque farms and barns will put you in Lancaster County, home to the horse-and-buggy Amish. Ever seen the movie *Witness*? Just for the record, there really are towns there with names like Bird-in-Hand and Intercourse." They both laughed, and the would-be guide's narrative travelogue reached its ending.

Sydney searched inwardly for what she hoped would be an understandable and acceptable explanation for what she was sure must have been interpreted as inexcusable, perhaps unforgivable, behavior. She thought it might be easier to first explain to Isa, who had told her she wouldn't just hand over Mena's number or contact information until she was convinced Sydney was sincere, the story she told was true, and that doing so wouldn't set back Mena. From where they sat today, Sydney assured Isa she'd learned from her past, worked on it in the present, and was ready for a future she hoped would include Mena.

"You know, I had just returned to counseling not long before Mena's accident. I had finally admitted to myself that I had a problem with intimacy and relationships. It's a long story, not worth a bother right now. But this one is. I have a penchant for believing in signs, omens, prescient sentiment, if you will. For days before you called to tell me about Mena's accident, she had come back to me in my thoughts and memory. I was at a loss for explaining why until your call. Then it all made sense to me. You see, Mena and I had a different kind of relationship from the start. Different in that we first connected on a level that superseded all pretenses, looks, sexual chemistry, whatever it is that draws one person to another. Our attraction was intellectual, emotional, I guess you could say. We shared an interest in human anthropology, history, cultures, peoples, languages, literatures, writing. Of course, I shouldn't and can't speak for her. That's merely the way I understood what happened between us. Whatever it was, it was, for want of a more aptly descriptive word, magical. To me, anyway."

Sydney spent more than two hours that day recounting her past with Mena to Isa.

"IT ALL SOUNDS SO ROMANTIC."

"Oddly, I never thought of it that way, but our different ways of seeing things had been part of our problem. I admit, at the time, I foolishly didn't even try to put myself in her place. If I'm to be completely honest, I'd go as far as to say that I then thought her views and affairs of the heart were ridiculously reminiscent of a child's fantasy."

"What made you change your mind?"

"After she left, and with a little help from a professional friend, I saw that I had not only stopped feeling, but I no longer believed. I'd hardened my heart to protect it from breaking, and although I hadn't been aware at the time, it was again softening thanks to and because of Mena. I had become a stodgy old academic, a curmudgeon insensate. It wasn't until Mena had left me all alone that I realized how much I truly loved her. Despite all I'd done to prevent it, my heart was so painfully aching."

"I've read some of your writing. Your novel, the book that reached out to Mena. I can see what she saw in it. Maybe not to the depths she did, but no unfeeling being could have written what you did. There's so much love in your pages. She saw it. It touched her. Maybe you just needed another to help you navigate your loneliness, to bring those feelings out again."

"We shared the common bonds of intellect and cerebral yearnings, yet we differed in many other important ways. I am, at the core of my being, much more of an introverted loner. Of course, I have to interact with others in my profession, but I end up drained afterward and need solitude in order to recover. Mena couldn't understand that, my need to be alone. Her want and need was quite the contrary. Although she, too, is a loner at heart, she's much more of an extrovert in that she needs to reach out to at least one other. She thrives on such togetherness. I, on the other hand, felt smothered by the constant attention. I had hoped we could come to an understanding of each other, that what we'd found, what had brought us together, would at least…" Sydney stopped mid-sentence and said, "Anyway, it doesn't matter now."

"But of course, it does," Isa countered. "Isn't that *really* why I'm here? Why you called and invited me to come? I mean, while I'm looking forward to the chance to see all those wonderful places you painted such compelling pictures of, you didn't really ask me here simply so you could show me around. C'mon, I'm not that naive. You have to admit to yourself that you still love her. Very much."

Sydney's head snapped up, as if a deep, dark secret that had been buried for years had just been uncovered. Then her face relaxed into acceptance of not wanting to hide her feelings anymore, especially from herself.

"Yes. Yes, I do. For what it's worth. But I'm not sure I didn't ruin my chances by disappearing again without an explanation."

"But you have an explanation, Mena just doesn't know it yet." Isa smiled weakly, in an attempt to lighten the intensity of the conversation. "I don't know. Maybe I'm a poor judge of all of this. I've never felt that kind of love for anyone, or from anyone. I can only imagine it's what everyone dreams of. Yet, how does a love that strong die? Or does it? Where do such feelings go? I can't believe you can ever get over something, someone, who's reached such a depth in your soul. I've been with Mena, I've seen her struggle with her ghosts and demons. If I were you, I wouldn't give up hope without a fight. Let me tell you a little secret of my own. Mena and I made love one night… We had sex. I'd been drinking, and Mena was so emotionally upset over something. I never knew what, but she just up and left in the middle of the night. She was terribly distraught, and I can't help but think it was because I was the first one, and it was the first time she'd been with anyone after you."

Sydney's eyes shimmered and grew wide. What Isa didn't know was that Sydney, far from having given up, was about to go all out in her attempt to win back Mena's heart. She decided now was the time to tell her. She started by divulging the *real* reason she'd asked Isa to come.

Isa had no idea what to say when Sydney was done revealing all. She wasn't sure how Mena would respond when she found out. Afraid for them both, she thought she should encourage, almost demand, that Sydney tell her before it was too late. But wasn't it already? After all, Mena had struggled to understand why Sydney had come and gone, leaving in her wake another hurtful five months filled with pain and confusion.

She broached the subject with Sydney, "Don't you think you should let her know? I really don't think you should keep this big of a secret."

"I just don't think it's the kind of thing that can be done over the phone. It'll only be a few more weeks. I'll be moved and settled in by Christmas."

The reality of that awareness sunk in for both women as they each retreated into themselves and the silence of their own thoughts.

Finally, Isa spoke. "I know the day will come when I'll feel like shit for doing this, but it has to be done." She handed Sydney a few printer pages stapled together. "I guess you've never seen this?"

"I don't think so. What is it?" She looked at the title page. "No, I haven't."

"Mena just showed it to me a few months ago. She was about to throw it out, but I managed to salvage it from the trash."

Sydney glanced again at it.

Isa handed it to her. "You should read it. It's your story, you know? Mena wrote it as a sort of healing, some therapy, I guess. Although it details a few of your differences, I think you'll find that you two have a lot in common."

Sydney's forehead creased.

"Not the smallest example of which is the very existence of this story. I doubt she would ever open up like this to just anyone. Maybe that's why she never sent it in after writing it. Like you, she reveals her heart and soul by way of written words, on paper. It works for her, and for you too. Seems like the lesson here might be that you should continue to write to each other, even when you're close enough to talk."

Isa smiled at Sydney, who asked, "Can I hold onto this for a while?"

"Of course. Like I said, it's yours. You need to read it. It'll help you understand Mena's side of your story. Can you just maybe wait to answer if she asks how you figured all this out?" After being made privy to the very personal and private messages written into Mena's "Love at first write," Isa felt like she'd been given a directive and was meant to serve as an intermediary between these two women, who needed someone to help push and pull them together. Otherwise, it may never happen.

Mena was still in love with Sydney and probably always would be. And Isa had a good idea the feelings were equally returned. She did it to help their relationship, and Sydney, who she was really starting to like, know, understand, and see differently.

Together, they devised a plan they hoped would work.

CHAPTER 17

As the Christmas season approached, Mena prepared herself and her classes for two glorious weeks of vacation. She read the younger children the holiday tale *Pancho's Piñata* and helped them make their own similar candy- and toy-filled clay pots and star-shaped creations, which they would break open at their own Fiestas Navideñas. She then introduced the older students to both Mexican and Spanish traditions. First, Las Posadas, the recreation of Mary and Joseph's journey in search of an inn where she could give birth to Jesus. These days, the emphasis was more on the party that would take place when they finally reached the house that would allow them in. Another favorite was las uvas a las doce, the December 31st tradition of eating one grape for each chime of a midnight clock announcing a new year and a new day.

It was a fun and festive time for all. Even Mena, maybe most of all.

The joy of the season was in the Yankee Candle- and balsam fir-scented air, reaching its peak at the party on the last day before the winter break. Over punch and cookies, the students thanked their teacher for making learning enjoyable and lavished her with homemade cards and handcrafted gifts, the ones she treasured most of all.

Lupe gave her a tote bag full of new picture books for reading days in future classes, and Magda parted with one of her worry dolls.

"This one works the best," Magda said, "if you whisper your worries in her ear, low, so that no one else can hear, before you put her under your pillow when you go to bed. She'll scare them far away so you can have sweet dreams."

Mena smiled. It was the girl's version of what she had told them about the origin of the small, brightly colored figures.

Itziar gave her a piece of pottery she'd made in art class, a glazed clay star. "For your Christmas tree at home," she said.

And Mateo drew her a picture of her own Chesa and Emi. He knew what they looked like because she had photos of them on her desk in their classroom.

"It's beautiful," she said. Using magnets, she hung it on her file cabinet right away.

Before they knew it, the last bell rang, signaling the start of their vacation. "Yay!" They yelled in excitement as they packed up Mena's gifts to them—spoils from the piñata and whatever candy and cookie crumbs remained on their plates—and headed out the door.

It was time for Mena to go home, pack up her fur babies, and head back to Flagstaff with Isa to check the cameras she'd left there and do more unofficial investigating. Not wanting to take advantage of Alex's generosity, they'd decided to rent a cabin of their own this time. She'd let Isa make all the arrangements.

"You're being unusually quiet," Mena said to Isa. "Are you feeling okay?"

Isa swallowed the lump that had formed in her throat as they passed a sign for the Surprise exit off Highway 17. Somehow, she didn't think Mena would appreciate the segue. But as the miles passed by, the clock ticked. She needed to find the courage to tell her about the real surprise that was coming.

Although she wasn't at all hungry, Isa's stomach had been tied in knots to rival the one in her throat since they'd pulled away, she said, "I need some food, Mena. Is it okay if we stop for something to eat?"

Wrinkles appeared across Mena's forehead. "Sure. At the next exit? Did you have something in mind? A place you'd already scoped out? I must admit, I'm kinda surprised you're hungry."

"Why? Aren't you?"

"No, but maybe I ate more than you did for breakfast. I guess I just assumed you'd fill up before we set out."

"Sorry. I didn't really feel like eating then. Anywhere's fine." Isa made herself small in the seat.

Mena drove on until they saw a few restaurant signs and exited at a place called Black Canyon City and headed for Nora Jean's Koffee Kitchen.

Isa waited until their food was brought to the table before she told Mena everything.

The woman's silence in response was killing her.

"Mena, please say something. I only just found out myself at Thanksgiving. I didn't know, I swear."

"But you *did* know about *this* surprise. You planned it, even. Were you really going to let me pull up to her place, thinking it was a rental property we'd be living in for a week, without telling me? Can you imagine how I'm feeling right now?"

Mena didn't even know how she was feeling herself. She'd tried to avoid thinking about Sydney ever since she'd appeared by her hospital bed, only to again disappear without her promised goodbye. It all seemed so strange. "Funny thing is, now it all seems to make sense." She laughed. "It's almost like what I did when I moved to be with her. It was spontaneous, she said so herself. Said she hadn't had time to prepare for it." She laughed again. "Paybacks sure are hell."

She looked across the table at Isa, and despite her unhappiness with the way this was being sprung on her, she realized she was being a little harsh with and unfair to her friend. Isa was only trying to help. She decided to give her a break.

"Well, I guess it's fitting that I'm finding out here."

Isa looked at her with narrowed eyes.

"We *are* on the edge of the Tonto National Forest, and I'm feeling a little tonta right now for having been so played." A smile of a genuine nature spread widely across Mena's face. "But a little warning would have been nice." She sat her coffee down and looked at Isa.

She wasn't quite ready to meet Sydney again, heart to heart and face to face, so she had Isa call and tell her they'd be arriving a day late. She needed time to think about what she wanted to say and to prepare herself for the flash flood she feared would rise over her after the opening of the emotional floodgates.

"You're gonna pay for this, mi'jita," Mena playfully said before snatching the ticket off the table. "And I'm not talking about this check for our breakfast either." She waved the register receipt in her face.

They drove on to Sedona but stopped at the first hotel they'd come upon after exiting onto Highway 179, the Hilton Sedona Resort at Bell Rock. It looked like a nice enough place. Mena faked like she was going to make Isa pay for their stay. After all, they had said they'd share the cost of the cabin they were supposed to have been renting. *Let her sweat it a little bit.* She'd pick up the tab in the morning.

After they checked in, put their bags in the room, and fed Emi and Chesa, it was time to start talking. Mena really didn't want to leave the hotel. All she needed was to run into Sydney out there before she was ready. She walked to the window and looked out at the scenery. It was such a beautiful place. She hadn't really been able to enjoy the area before. All she'd seen of it then was black and burned. With the sun out and shining on the red rocks, the sight was majestic, captivating. She really wanted to get out in it. *What the hell?* They could walk and talk, and unless Sydney had changed, she wouldn't be out hiking the trails. She'd likely be cooped up inside writing, anyway.

THE NEXT MORNING FOUND MENA energized and ready for whatever feelings might come.

As they pulled up outside of Sydney's place, she quipped, "Just what is it with northerners? They all seem to have a cabin. Even though, no surprise, this one seems to be luxurious too." Mena shook her head, trying to lighten the mood and distract herself from more serious thoughts she knew were coming.

From somewhere on the other side of the Jeep, maybe from inside the house, she thought she heard a dog bark. Chesa had heard it too and was already responding in her own canine language with expressly excited tail-wagging.

"Jenny?" Mena couldn't believe it. She turned and saw the sheltie, who shyly kept her distance while approaching slowly, sniffing all the way. "It's me, girl! Don't tell me you've forgotten me? Get over here and let me love on you!" Mena crouched and opened her arms to the dog. Finally, after much barking and lots more sniffing, Jenny must have caught a scent she recognized. She lunged into Mena's arms, licking and nuzzling her with her muzzle. "Oh, my sweet girl. I've missed you so much."

So caught up in her homecoming with the pup she'd given up on ever seeing again, Mena hadn't yet looked up to where the human, whose voice she heard coming from the porch above, stood waiting. Truth be told, she wasn't ready for what was to come, and she was content where she was: on the ground, out of sight, playing with the dogs. Hiding.

But she knew she couldn't avoid the inevitable for much longer, so she got up and dusted off her jeans. The moment she saw Sydney, her heart flipped into cartwheels beneath the button-down covering her chest. The traitor. No longer numb and drugged as she was during her hospital daze, the enormity of feeling hit her unexpectedly hard.

Isa slipped around their hostess and disappeared inside, giving Sydney and Mena some privacy.

"Hello, Mena."

"Sydney."

"You're looking well. Completely recovered, I hope?"

"All better now."

"That's great. I'm not sure how to get over this small talk, but as I recall, the last time I saw you, we were deep in an important conversation."

"Yes, and best I can remember, I wasn't doing much of the talking."

"I hope we find some time to start again where we left off. Then and in that long ago February."

"So do I."

"I've missed you, Mena. I'm so happy that you came."

As much as she wanted to, Mena couldn't say all she was feeling. She hoped those words would unlock themselves from where she had them—for now, in a well-guarded chamber.

Thankfully, it wasn't long before Jenny reappeared to demand more of Mena's undivided attention. With the dancing dog and the delicious aromas emanating out the open door from what she expected would be a magnificent chef's kitchen, her heart was soon quieted by her stomach's awakening. She'd almost forgotten what a good cook Sydney was.

With massive cast iron skillets lined up across the top of what appeared to be a six-burner Viking range, she and Isa were detoured to an island covered with a myriad of omelet makings. In a glance, she saw mushrooms, ham, cheese, and spinach. She also saw sausage links and bacon that was crisp, the only way she liked it. *Of course, Sydney would have known and remembered*. To the side of that culinary station, she caught glimpses of bagels and cream cheese, a variety of other fresh baked breads, toast, juice, and coffee. There was far too much on the smorgasbord for the three of them to eat in a week.

"Sweet baby Jesus! And I thought your place in Maryland was over the top. I hope you're planning on hosting lots of parties here," Isa said in appreciation.

Mena smiled at the memory and looked at Sydney. "I remember how distraught you were to find that your exquisite new home had an electric range and not a gas one."

Now it was Sydney's turn to laugh. "You know, I almost backed out of the deal because of it." She held Mena's gaze.

Oh God. There it is. That look, that feeling she was trying to hold at bay. Mena looked away, but not soon enough.

AFTER THEY'D STUFFED THEMSELVES TO the point where not another crumb could be eaten, Isa, to remind them she was still there, offered,

"That was magnificent, Sydney. The best brunch I've ever had. Compliments to the chef." She raised her glass of OJ in homage to the hostess of the meal and gave it a three-star Michelin rating.

Mena spoke from experience, "If you think that was something, just wait." She winked at Sydney as if the two of them shared a secret, which they did.

Sydney explained, "Yes, dinners can be much more fun to prepare than brunches."

"Well, in that case, would it be too bold of me to say I can't wait?"

All three of them had a good laugh at the eagerness of Isa's earnestness and in anticipation of what was to come, despite their currently full stomachs.

As Mena and Isa moved to clear the counters and pick things up, however, Sydney stopped them. "That can wait. I want you to see the rest of my home." She looked Mena in the eye when she said, "*Mi casa es su casa*. C'mon. I'm not quite finished unpacking and moving in, but I want to hear what you think."

A WHILE LATER, ISA LOOKED at both of them and said, "If you don't mind, I'm gonna take Chesa for a walk. I don't think it would be wise to let her out off-leash in such a beautiful, unknown place. All we need is for her to go after a squirrel and find herself unable to make it back home. Besides, I need to waddle some of this newly acquired weight off if I'm going to pack more on later this evening. I would ask you to join me, but I think you need to catch up and get yourselves reacquainted."

Sydney mouthed the words that Mena spoke. "Thanks, Isa."

The door had barely closed behind her when Sydney seized the gauntlet. "Do you feel any differently now, Mena? Now that you know my past of which you'd been unaware?"

Mena took her time answering. "Not because of it. I always knew you were very spiritual. I just didn't know quite how religious. Now that I do, it makes me wonder what you think of me, of us. What that would look like going forward. In a relationship."

"Mena, that was a long time ago. Years before you and I were ever together the first time. I'd come to terms with who I was well before then. That's why I left the order before taking my final vows. I knew in my heart why I'd entered the convent. I needed a safe place for healing and time to get to know me. By the time I finally got over Allyson, I realized it wouldn't be just her. It was me. I was attracted to women and wanted more than a 'particular friendship' in a convent. That was not the life for me."

"So that wasn't why you left our shared bedroom that day?"

"No, Mena. If only I had talked to you then like we're talking now."

"Why didn't you?"

"In all honesty, you didn't really give me a chance. You blew up immediately."

"I did, I admit it. I was afraid."

"Of…?"

"Losing you." Mena laughed, "Isn't it ironic?"

"Well, you haven't exactly lost me. We just had to go our separate ways until we could figure it out. I'm sure you've heard the phrase, 'If you love someone, you should set them free.'"

"And if they come back to you, then it was meant to be."

"And here we are." Sydney opened her arms and Mena moved in.

The comfort she'd felt from the very start was still there. All she had to do was remove the layers she'd put in place that separated them.

As promised, dinner did not disappoint. Isa didn't expect it would after finding all kinds of goodies in the gourmet space while putting food away and cleaning up the kitchen. Pullout drawers with ingredients that would have made the Spice Girls envious to a seemingly bottomless pantry and a freezer filled with enough contents to put any *Top Chef* contestant in the finals.

FIRESIDE THAT EVENING, SITTING IN the cool outdoors by the chiminea after their food had finally settled into a cramped space, Mena found herself listening to a conversation Sydney and Isa were having and wondered why it seemed like no time had passed since she and Sydney had been together. It all seemed so relaxed and easy, like the clock had stopped the moment she had walked out on that cold February day. *Is it because Isa is here?* The real test would come when she and Sydney were alone for an extended period, face to face.

Sydney interrupted Mena's thoughts by asking, "Would you like to see what I'm working on these days?" Without waiting for a response, she slid the first few chapters of a fledgling manuscript toward her across the table.

Mena scooted closer and began reading.

When she'd finished, Mena handed the pages back to Sydney and shook her head with a smile. "I guess some things never change."

Mena looked at Sydney to see her eyebrows raised and arched.

"Go back and look at what you, yourself, have written. You have the wrong two characters headed toward a relationship. Again. Remember the last time you asked my opinion on your writing? It should be Cyndi and Nena, not Nena and whoever that guy is. By the way, just where did you get those names from, anyway?"

Sydney returned her grin.

And that's when and how it all began, their writing together again.

IT WAS CHRISTMAS EVE, MENA'S favorite day of the year. Since she'd been a child, it was always the day of her biggest celebration. Religious significance aside, by Christmas Day, the exuberance of the secular holiday seemed significantly shallow in comparison. All the excitement, the buildup, reached its crescendo on the twenty-fourth. As they sat around the tree, engaged in reminiscing about holidays past and sharing stories about favorite foods and family traditions, Sydney surprised them each with a gift.

"It's not much, but I wanted to show my gratitude for your friendship."

Isa didn't hesitate when given the go-ahead to be the first to open her present, and exclaimed, "Oh my God! These are wonderful. You are amazing. Thank you so much."

"I saw you admiring them the other day and got the impression they might be a little out of the price range for a struggling student, so you helped a clueless Santa out. Thank *you*."

Isa popped in the AirPods and stood to hug Sydney.

After settling back into the sofa, she turned toward Mena, who was just about to unwrap her box, when Isa startled them by nearly screaming, "Wait! This moment calls for some music, and I've got just the song. I brought it along." She hurried off to her room and quickly returned. "It's not a traditional carol or holiday tune, but it's a classic contemporary and one of my favorites," she prepped them before Celine Dion's "Don't Save it All for Christmas Day" played. "Appropriate, wouldn't you say?" By all appearances, she was quite pleased with herself.

"Now can I open my present?" Mena teased.

Isa laughed. "Sure, go ahead, what are you waiting for?"

Mena looked first at her, then at Sydney, before slowly and agonizingly removing the beautiful foil wrapping from the square box in her hand. With the ribbon undone, she lifted the lid and looked inside. There, atop a protective pillow of cotton, rested a small, circular, gold medallion with an exquisitely rendered image of the Patron Saint of Firefighters engraved in its center and the prayer *Saint Florian Protect Us* etched around its perimeter.

Her heart flooded. "It's perfect, Sydney. I love it. Thank you." She risked a glance at the giver before lifting it out of the box for a closer look and passing it to Isa. Not realizing the box wasn't yet empty, she set it aside with the discarded wrapping.

"Don't you know you should *always* look under the filler?" Sydney hinted with a smile directed Mena's way.

With a curious quirk to her mouth and expression in her eyes, Mena reached for the box and removed the fluffy contents the medal rested upon. Her heart expanded trifold when there within she found the gold chain both she and Sydney had worn.

"It belongs to you, Mena. I gave it to you with all my heart. Please keep it this time."

Mena struggled with heavy emotion as Isa rose from her place and removed both pieces of jewelry from the box. Carefully threading the necklace's links through the bail, she draped the chain over Mena's neck and securely fastened it in place.

"Oh!" Sydney's cry startled them both. "I almost forgot." She left the room and quickly returned with what looked like a few cards. She handed them each one.

While Mena chose to read hers in silence, Isa read hers aloud.

"Oh, Almighty God, whose great power
and eternal wisdom embraces the universe,
watch over all firefighters.
Protect them from harm in the
performance of their duty to fight fire,
save lives, and preserve property.
We pray, help them to keep our homes and
all buildings safe day and night.
We recommend them to Your loving care
because their duty is dangerous.
Grant them Your unending strength and
courage in their daily assignments.
Dear God, protect these brave persons.
Grant them Your almighty protection and
unite them safely with their families after
duty has ended.
Amen."

"It's the Firefighter's Prayer to St. Florian," Sydney explained. "I wanted you each to have one. Someday, I'd like to show you both the lovely chapel where I found them."

"I think I can speak for both of us," Isa shared with a smile. "We'd love to see what so inspires you, to know that part of you. As friends, and because we love you, what's important to you is important to us."

EVERYTHING WAS GOING SO WELL that they decided to throw together an impromptu get-together for New Year's Eve and were surprised at the number of people who said they'd be happy to come. Though the crew was used to roughing it, it helped that there were cabins available in the Red Rock Ranger District, and that Alex had offered up her B and B. It wasn't hard to entice visitors to Sedona. It was a place everyone wanted to visit, given a reason and opportunity. Since Christmas gatherings with extended families were over, it was perfect.

Sydney, of course, was ecstatically in her culinary element. The spread was no less than delectably divine, as was the bubbly Dom Perignon and proffered wine. The first round had trays filled with baked cranberry brie, smoked salmon dip, and guacamole deviled eggs circulating throughout the house. Round two consisted of mouthwatering offerings of spinach puffs, chicken bacon ranch pinwheels, three-bite tacos with avocado cream, and honey garlic meatballs.

One thing was for sure: no one here would ring in the New Year on an empty stomach.

Small groups and pairs scattered inside and out. Judging by the laughter and looks on their faces, all seemed to be having a great time. Joe and Traci were there, as was Mike Davila. Most of the fire crew— Gonzalez, Selitto, Larsen, and Castillo—had shown up with dates or spouses. Even Alex made an appearance, though she couldn't stay for the ball drop. All were happy to see Mena again, some more than a little curious to know her connection to the hostess and owner of such a grand house.

By two in the morning, those who were leaving had already gone, while a few guests, who'd no doubt be ushering in the first day of the year nursing gargantuan hangovers, insisted on staying to help with clean-up and to partake of the promised morning mimosas. But when even Isa, who'd left with Mike to catch a flight to Vegas where she'd promised to meet up with her family for a late celebration of the holidays had gone, Sydney and Mena finally found themselves alone together for the first time.

Without words, they joined hands and hearts and mustered up enough energy to slow dance to, of all things, a Lady Gaga song, and they spent the remainder of the week holding each other and making up for lost time with "Always Remember Us This Way" on a loving repeat.

CHAPTER 18

By the time March rolled around and Mena had another school break, she and Isa again packed their bags and prepared to head north. This time, they hoped to get a little camping and kayaking in before the scorch of summer and subsequent fire season demanded they return to work.

Although she and Sydney had seen each other a few times since January, they had vowed to take it slower this time. To say Mena was surprised when Sydney expressed an interest in joining them would have been an understatement of a colossal size.

"I'm sorry. I had no idea you'd want to come along, Syd. We only have two kayaks."

"Oh. I guess I don't know how this works. No worries, I'll go next time." She put on a good front, but disappointment rang loud and clear in the timbre of her voice.

"That's not necessary. I'm sure we can rent a tandem someplace." Mena looked at Isa, who immediately pulled out her phone and began searching. After finding and securing one that was at a place on their way, Sydney packed lunches consisting of peanut butter and jelly sandwiches, some pretzels, cookies, fruit, and water. Their camping gear was already stowed, and they'd stop for more provisions and ice for the Yeti somewhere on the road.

"Does everyone have a hat and jacket?" Mena asked. "Better safe and warm than sorry and cold." She checked to make sure the boats were secure one last time before the trio pulled away and out the gate.

They'd decided to put in at the Beasley Flat Access Point on the Verde River, which they'd been promised offered both rapids and flat water paddling with ledge drops and walled turns divided by calm waters, replete with opportunities for rest and relaxation. Mena'd been told the locals call it The Dirty Verde, but she'd never found a sandy or muddy body of water to detract from the natural beauty of a place. *To each their own*, she thought.

By the time they reached their destination, what few clouds had been in the sky had given way to the promise of a beautiful day. Mena passed out the life vests, put hers on, and stretched upward to untie the kayaks before reminding them, "Don't forget your hats and jackets and sunscreen, or whatever else you think you might want or need."

With the two-seater down from the roof, Mena and Isa carried it to the water's edge. As Isa went back for hers, Mena asked Sydney, "Front or back?" Not that she was going to give her a choice; she just wanted to hear what she'd say.

"Well, if I get to choose, I suppose sitting in the front would offer the best view."

Mena nodded, all the while knowing that's where she'd put her no matter what she'd said. The experienced and stronger paddler always sat in the back, taking on the role of the helmsman. Sydney was much better suited as the scenery lookout.

Before they pushed out, she reminded Sydney they needed to be in sync while paddling, in unison, with their oars in the water on the same alternating side. Unsure she understood, Mena said, "Don't worry. Just paddle on the left, then on the right. Where you lead, I shall follow. The goal is to not clash and struggle against one another." *Hmm, that sounds familiar.*

Once they were afloat, Mena leaned forward to better hear what she thought Sydney was saying. "This is so much better than a canoe. It seems less likely to tip over, and it's much nicer not to have to lift the oar up out of the water and across the boat from side to side."

"You mean this isn't your first time out in a boat?" Mena thought back to their island adventures and Sydney's self-professed manic fear of drowning.

"Well, I haven't actually ever *been* in a canoe, but I have placed others there in my writing. In my mind, it's almost the same," she laughed.

They explored the river for the better part of three hours, steering clear of the rapids, since it was Sydney's first time. Afterward, they headed for shore to grab a bite to eat before continuing the day's journey.

"I don't know about you two," Isa said as she tore into one of the brown paper sacks that held their food, "but I'm starving."

"Slow down, girl!" Mena laughed. "Don't worry. Remember, Sydney made extras."

"Oh, yeah." She immediately reached into the basket and grabbed another one.

Mena shook her head with a smile on her face. "Comelona," she called her playfully.

As they devoured their bag lunches, they enjoyed the peace, quiet, and surrounding scenery. Mena checked the time, wanting to reach their final destination before it got too late, and packed things up while Isa and Sydney sat a little longer, leaning back into the warmth of the sun.

The second part of their adventure would take them to Manzanita at Oak Creek. The campground itself was about an hour away from where they were now and another hour from where they'd be headed in the morning.

From the driver's seat, Mena shook her head again in disbelief. "Sydney, I still can't believe you've fallen so far from your accustomed four-star, luxury room service providing accommodations to tent camping, not even bridging the gap with an RV. What happened?"

"Sometimes you just gotta go with the flow." She turned her head to wink at Isa, who she'd thanked more than four months earlier for sharing Mena's written story and how she'd felt about giving up all that she loved.

As soon as they reached their site, Mena showed them both how to lay the tent out on the ground, assemble the poles, and drive the stakes. Although they weren't expecting any rain, she even had Isa help her dig a small trench around the perimeter of the canvas floor to help keep water out and them dry, just in case there'd been a meteorological mistake.

Having accomplished that goal, Mena realized they'd lost a camper somewhere along the way: Sydney. *Where did she go?* Mena wondered, yet she continued preparing their sleeping quarters for the night to come, saving for later her lectures regarding the importance of keeping their sleeping bags rolled until it was time to climb inside and ensure the zippered door flap was always completely closed.

Fait accompli. When they'd finished setting up, Mena and Isa walked the surrounding area, where they stumbled upon a lounging Sydney, her nose stuck deep in a book.

"Shouldn't you be writing, not reading?" Mena admonished her jokingly.

Sydney smiled.

They insisted she put the book down and join them for a sunset hike and some wildflower hunting. "It's my turn to dole out some laminated cards," Mena shared as she gave one to Sydney and another to Isa.

"Wow!" Isa exclaimed. "These are beautiful. At least, in pictures."

Mena nodded in agreement before challenging, "Let's see who can find the most. But don't pick them, just call for buddy verification. Better yet, pic them." She held up her camera. "Always treat nature responsibly and respectfully."

They started off in different directions, but before they got too far, Mena called out a cautionary reminder, "And don't forget to mark your trail. We don't need anyone getting lost out here today."

Looking down at the card she held in her hands, Sydney commented to Isa, "Unfortunately, it looks like not all of them will be in bloom yet. It's too early. But according to this, we might find some larkspur and lupine. Columbine, however, won't likely make an appearance for another couple of weeks."

"Guess we'll just have to come back," was Isa's solution to that.

"Yes, we will. I've already decided that monkshood is my personal favorite, and we won't find that botanical beauty until June or much later."

That evening, when the stars came out, they roasted marshmallows on sticks and made s'mores. After they'd stuffed themselves with sweetness, Mena incessantly rechecked and doused the fire with water to the top of the metal ring, only then deeming it safe. She wasn't, however, so sure about their sleeping arrangements. She'd intentionally worked it so she'd be the last one in the tent, letting Sydney and Isa decide who'd spend the night where. When she finally worked up the courage to unzip the flap, she found she would be sleeping in the middle. *This should be interesting and fun*, she thought. It really wasn't uncomfortable at all. Each woman stayed in her own space, no doubt exhausted from the day's activities, allowing Mena to relax and sleep peacefully.

ON THEIR LAST PLANNED DAY at Sydney's cabin, Mena, as usual, was the first one up and around. Sydney had preprogrammed the coffee maker the night before, so Mena was happy to find a fresh pot waiting. She turned some music on low, so it wouldn't bother the others, and stood looking out the window as Adele sang "Set Fire to the Rain."

She was surprised when Sydney's voice interrupted the singing from behind her.

"You know you can, right?"

Mena looked over her shoulder before pouring herself another cup. With a gesture, she asked Sydney if she wanted one.

She nodded and whispered, "Please."

"I know I can…what?" Mena turned to face Sydney and handed her the coffee.

"Stay here forever."

Mena looked at her questioningly.

"I know this song."

Mena looked at her again, just in time to see a single, solitary tear leave a track down her face.

They had a little time alone before Isa woke up, and they used it to talk about what a life together for them might look like. How it would have to be different if they were to try. They both knew they could never again have what once was. That time of their life, that magic, was gone. But undeniably, the love was still there. It had survived, and it was strong, maybe stronger than ever. They agreed they both needed more time.

Meanwhile, Sydney left to shower and Mena stepped out to her Jeep.

It wasn't long before Isa joined her in the driveway, and as she looked at the papers and notes Mena was going through, she remembered something. "I never told you he came to see you when you were in the hospital."

"Henderson?"

"Yeah. It was weird. I found him talking to you while you were still out, before you came around. He was even crying, if you can believe that."

"Maybe his conscience was getting the best of him. Look, I know I shouldn't say anything without proof, but I'm not sure I don't have it." Mena told Isa what she'd found in the incident reports and on the images captured by the deer cams.

Isa looked at her. Was it with disbelief, or was it hurt that she'd been left out until now? It was hard for Mena to tell.

"I'm still searching. That's the real reason I wanted to come back here. I just can't believe, I don't want to believe, that someone we know, someone on our crew, could do such a thing. The thing is, I'm not sure he's been doing it all on his own." Mena looked at Isa imploringly. "I'm trusting you with this until I figure out what we've got. Please don't tell anyone, Isa. Not even Mike."

"Did I just hear my name taken in vain?"

Isa, who'd made arrangements for Mike to join them, ran to him and wrapped him in a hug.

Mena greeted him and gave the two of them some space by joining Sydney, dressed and ready to go—*and looking pretty good, for that matter*—waiting on the porch with the laptop open. The split screen showed recorded image numbers with date and time stamps, as well as descriptions.

Mena leaned over her shoulder. "Looks like you've been busy. Have you found anything interesting or worth telling me about?"

"You tell me." Sydney pointed to the screen, "Looks like the same man in the same vehicle keeps showing up."

Mena knew without looking who the man was. He'd been on her radar all along. It was time to take her suspicions and all she'd compiled in the way of proof and evidence to Peña.

"I KNOW HOW THIS LOOKS and is sure to sound, but please, Chief, hear me out."

Mena told and showed him everything she'd found.

Peña didn't say anything for a long while, causing Mena to fear she'd stepped far out of bounds. Still, she held her ground, until he looked up from the accusations and confirmation laid out on the desktop and sighed loudly. He looked at her as if considering what to do, then, using a key on a chain he pulled from deep in his pocket, he bent to unlock a drawer and took out a nondescript, unmarked file and passed it her way.

"I would have told you if I could have," he said to her, almost as an apology as she opened the manila folder, her eyes drawn to a familiar name. "We've suspected him for quite some time. We just didn't have enough to nail him, but the truth caught up to him in Flagstaff."

Mena had to know, "The Elden Fire?"

Peña nodded. "I guess it finally became too personal, nearly cost you your life. And that realization must have got to him somewhere deep inside. One day, he just lost it, broke down completely, and told me everything."

"Did he say how many? Which ones? Did he say why?"

"He confessed to three or four by name. I'm sure there were more. Hopefully, it will all come out in time. He never really gave a reason. He had some anger issues, even had some rage going on. We suspect it was a combination of that and his need, or greed, for the constant flow of hazard pay it brought in. Love and money are usually the catalysts for all crimes."

"So what happens now?"

"Oh, he's definitely going to do some time."

"Jeez, it's no secret I never liked the guy, but—"

"Don't even go there, Mendoza. He doesn't deserve your sympathy. He betrayed the brotherhood. He betrayed us. He could have killed people. His actions destroyed homes and caused millions of dollars in damage. He put all our lives in danger. My only regret is that we couldn't stop him sooner."

Mena nodded in agreement and started toward the door. She hesitated before turning the knob, however, and spun back around.

"I guess now maybe isn't the best time for another matter I need to discuss?"

Peña dropped his head into his hands for the second time during their visit. "Go ahead. Whatever it is, lay it on me. I'm already numb."

Mena knew the sooner she told him the better.

"I'm moving."

At that revelation, Peña's head quickly jerked up.

"To where? And why? May I ask?"

"Only to Sedona. I'll still be able to help. And I'm thinking about going back to school. For arson investigation. You know what they say," she paused before smiling and finishing her thought, "*Everything happens for a reason.*"

"That's fantastic! You obviously have a knack for it, but don't think I don't know that's not the real, or at least the only, most compelling reason. You're avoiding the *why*, Mena." Peña sat back with a smile. "Let me help you out like I did that very first time you stepped into this office. Do you remember?"

Of course, she did.

"Tell me, does it have anything to do with love?"

Before she had a chance to answer, Peña laughed and said, "Forget it, Mendoza, you're busted. Your face just told me everything." He laughed again, louder this time.

Mena reached deep down for the courage to tell the man, "Well, maybe not quite everything."

WHEN SHE WAS FINISHED TELLING him her love and life stories, including revealing her sexual orientation, she was surprised by his response.

"Don't take this the wrong way, Mendoza, but Traci and I have known for a long time. We've just been waiting for you to feel comfortable enough to share that part of you with us."

A single tear—of relief, of happiness, of both—escaped her heart and found its way down her face to her shirt front.

"Oh, Mena." He got up from behind his desk and put his arms out for a hug.

She gladly stepped inside his embrace.

"Don't you know? Haven't you always known? I love you just the way you are. And you're the only woman I can show affection to, other than my mother, without fear of my wife's retaliation." They shared a laugh and Mena had never felt freer and more relieved.

CHAPTER 19

THE ELDEN FIRE, WHEN ALL was said and done, had burned thousands of acres and required the assistance of hundreds of firefighters, including engine crews, helicopters, and backfiring, using both handheld drip torches and helitack units in charge of aerial ignition.

Although she had come a long way since the day of her accident, Mena knew before she could go any further, she'd have to first go back to that day and place, to where her old life had ended and her new one began.

Unable to bring herself to follow the exact route she had taken on that fateful morning, she drove to where Isa and Mike had parked their vehicles instead. She knew this only because of what they'd told her. All that remained of the lookout tower was a few structural beams and a slab of concrete where the foundation had been poured decades ago.

The charred remains that Mike and Joe had described from their last visit were just as they had said, as she had imagined. As strong as the pungent pines had been, all that was left in the air was a lingering scent of burnt wood and ash. The place was a desolate wasteland. It looked like the aftermath of a nuclear holocaust. The quiet was penetrating, to the extent it sent shivers down her spine and put bumps on her arms. She shook off the eerie feeling and forced herself to face what was left of the surrounding forest.

Remarkably, most of the large trees were still standing tall amidst weaker saplings that had bowed to the force of the fire and fallen. The survivors wore blackened battle scars on their bark, like a wounded soldier wears his Purple Heart. Mena looked up from the bottom of their trunks and inwardly saluted them. She marveled at their strength, fortitude, and resilience. In the bold, yet humbled way of a private who lacks the character and experience of a veteran, she dared compare what she'd been through to their bravery and suffering.

Love, like fire, can be equally explosive, volatile, and unpredictable. Cupid's arrow, like a lightning bolt, can hit an unsuspecting target dead-on and strike the very heart of it. The fire that ignites has several courses it can then take. Lacking fuel or oxygen, it will do little more than smoke and smolder, and it will quickly die out. At the opposite extreme, it can burn out of control and destroy everyone and everything it meets. What is hoped for is a slow burn, one that will allow itself to be tamed and directed. Such fires can be good for both humans and nature, allowing forests to rid themselves of fuels that have built up over time, giving lovers time to dispose of unnecessary baggage piece by piece, freeing themselves from the causes of blowups and the threat of irreparable harm to relationships.

Mena stooped and sifted through the remains at her feet, allowing the ashes to slip through her fingers as her mind sorted through the past year's happenings.

Tomorrow, she would return to Yuma to turn in her contract, unsigned, to the principal's secretary of the school where she'd been teaching. Although she'd sworn she'd never follow her heart in such a way again, she was willing to go the distance one more time, for Sydney, who'd proven her love and commitment to their relationship by doing the same and embracing change. She only hoped this time, they'd have their happy ending.

At the very moment of that thought, her attention was pulled away by the piercing *screech* of a hawk taking flight from a stalwart old growth tree. Like Pocahontas' Grandmother Willow, as Kim might say, this granddaughter of a wise Mother Nature had been around to witness the turning over of many new leaves in her day.

That was when she saw it.

A tiny blade of grass, barely noticeable, was struggling to break through the earth's burned blanket. She took it as a sign. One she had been looking for, what she needed. To her, it said and meant it would take time. But one day, this place, and she, would be teeming with life again. When that happened, both she and the cycle would be rejuvenated, renewed, whole, and complete.

She smiled, then headed for home.

 EPILOGUE

ITS ATTENTION TURNED TOWARD THE woodpecker's hammering in the otherwise still forest, the vermin failed to detect the rousing of a larger bird of prey, one with its eyes on the distracted prize on the forest floor. As the smaller bird continued to probe in search of bark beetles—insects that feast on the ponderosa pine's post-fire cambium laden with nutrients—animal instinct should have cautioned the creature to be careful, but the warning fell on ears deafened by the incessant boring. The flames of the blaze had thinned out the branches of the close-knit trees, dropping a pre-fire, previously impenetrable canopy of needles to the forest floor. Now able to clearly see its quarry, and with space to spread its wings and fly where it could do neither before, the hawk swooped downward, expertly navigating toward its food source. The mouse, with its beady eyes fixated on the fast-moving beak of the other, noisy bird, failed to see the predator until it was too late, its talons too close for escape. As the furry body was airlifted, the singular blade of grass in its vicinity moved almost indiscernibly on the ground's floor.

ACKNOWLEDGMENTS

MANY THANKS TO THE ENTIRE IP Team for seeing a "diamond in the rough" of my manuscript. Like the MCs in my pages, I hide my feelings well, so you may never know how much your belief in me and that first phone call really meant.

To Candy—for helping an old introvert navigate the world of tweeting and being social via online media. I'm a WIP, I admit ;) and for encouraging and inspiring me (not that you knew it at the time, but I've told you since) to try my hand at another genre via answering an early inquiry during the Interlude Press 2020 Tiny Book Fest.

To Choi—for *Wildfire's* beautiful cover. Its gorgeous simplicity has already been framed and hangs on my wall. I LOVE it!

and especially

To Annie—for helping me polish my writing to the best I could make it be. And for your hours of toil and sacrifice as my words like rocks, no doubt, tumbled through your head. Yet, you didn't give up on me.

I'm also extremely grateful to my sensitivity readers: Celeste Castro, Lucy Ibarra Podmore, Alex Perez, and Kimberly Zepeda for their insightful input and suggestions. Changes made to my story because of them greatly strengthened and vastly improved it.

ABOUT THE AUTHOR

TONI DRAPER WAS BORN AND lived most of her life in Maryland. These days, she calls home a two-acre sprawl in south Texas that she shares with her spouse, three rescued dogs, and a stray that stayed. *Wildfire* is her debut novel.

interludepress™

 interludepress.com
 @InterludePress
 interludepress
 store.interludepress.com

interlude  press,

you may also like...

Prize Money by Celeste Castro

Eva Angeles, a professional barrel racer, is saved mid-competition from a charging bull by Toma Rozene, an equestrian stuntwoman and bullfighter. Eva and Toma's shared passions and competitive spirits make friendship easy, but, as their feelings deepen, they must decide if the divergent futures they seek will stand in the way of love.

ISBN (print) 978-1-951954-03-1 | (eBook) 978-1-951954-04-8

Tack & Jibe by Lilah Suzanne

Willa documents a picture-perfect nautical life on Instagram, but when fans register her in a national sailing championship, she needs a crash course in sailing to protect her reputation. She gets help from champion sailor Lane Cordova, whose mastery of the sport is matched only by Willa's ineptitude—and her growing crush on Lane isn't helping matters. Can Willa keep her reputation afloat while taking a chance on love?

ISBN (print) 978-1-945053-93-1 | (eBook) 978-1-945053-94-8

Concerto in Chroma Major by Naomi Tajedler

Alexandra Graff is a stained-glass artist whose synesthesia gifts her with the ability to see sounds in colors. When she is hired to create glass panels for the new Philharmonie in Paris, she falls for Halina Piotrowski, a famous Polish pianist and helps her see the beauty that lies within her music.

ISBN (print) 978-1-945053-66-5 | (eBook) 978-1-945053-67-2